Strangeness in Sturgeon Book 1:

The Last Sin Eater

T. J. Lea

Copyright © 2021 T. J. Lea

All rights reserved.

The characters and events portrayed in this book are fictitious. Any similarity to real persons, living or dead, is coincidental and not intended by the author.

No part of this book may be reproduced, or stored in a retrieval system, or transmitted in any form or by any means, electronic, mechanical, photocopying, recording, or otherwise without written permission of the publisher.

Cover design by: Emily Houser

ISBN:
9798719637952

The Last Sin Eater

For my family, who I have been blessed to have so much borrowed time with.

For my friends and loved ones who ensured I never gave up until this was finally realised.

For Clara, who will live forever.

Contents

Preface — Pg 5

Prologue — Pg 6

The First Sin — Pg 8

The Second Sin — Pg 22

The Third Sin — Pg 34

The Fourth Sin — Pg 48

The Fifth Sin — Pg 61

The Sixth Sin — Pg 73

The Seventh Sin — Pg 81

The Final Sin — Pg 91

Epilogue — Pg 109

Acknowledgements — Pg 110

The Ferry of The Dead — Pg 114

Preface

I sit here, both at the beginning and the end of year one of "Stories Of Sturgeon." It is midnight on a Saturday and I am filled with unbelievable pride, shock, and fatigue… mostly fatigue, though undoubtedly not as much as my wonderful editor.

What you have in your hands, dear reader, is the culmination of a twenty year journey and the start of something wonderful:

The keys to Sturgeon.

This is the end result of sixteen months of planning, insomnia, highs and lows. Within these pages lie many conversations reflected in the world we see today—a world filled with ideologies that seek to divide and conquer. A world where the status quo is upheld at the expense of marginalised lives, and where the loudest, most aggressive voice in the room is the one people gravitate to. The voice filled with violence and hostility toward those who have done nothing to hurt them.

So it is all the more important to know how to combat it efficiently.

While there are otherworldly creatures tucked within these pages, the kinds of people we're about to meet are very, very real.

And it is up to us how we choose to handle them when meeting in the real world.

The Last Sin Eater is a journey that seeks not to glorify the inmates within the prison walls, but showcase them in the circles they created.

Every tale found within can have its roots traced to our world, to actual people.

It's all about that veil that separates us.

And how close we come to it every single day.

Prologue

This is the first of our chronicles within Sturgeon's walls and that of its people, but it is by no means the initial start of its troubles. You are simply witnessing a snapshot of the most important pairing in modern Sturgeon history. If you are new to this universe, you will require this section. If you are a long time reader, this will serve as a good refresher.

This town is unusual not solely because of its unmentionable location, but in that it sports a most unique housing arrangement. Nightmares live side by side (or as close as the barrier will allow) with both normal and "blighted" humans—those who possess unusual qualities as a mutation trait.

As you go through this series of tales, you will meet many unique individuals with their own ties to the complex ongoings of Sturgeon's underbelly. A bar between spaces that serves unique drinks with strange properties in exchange for the patron's stories, a hotel with innumerable floors housing all manner of horrific scenarios, an esteemed family with a long-standing tradition connected to the arcana, a group of teens gathered around a television set within the far reaches of Sturgeon, hiding a dark secret... and a tournament pitting some of the city's finest warriors against their nightmare counterparts, all in exchange for glory and a wish that will grant their deepest desires. A place where "the cycle" once again rears its ugly head. Old favourites return and new threats emerge as the threads of fate are tied together and the greater picture comes into focus.

This is where our first year ends.

There are many stories that intertwine our two main characters, but their tale begins here.

There is no story without Simon "Buck" McGraw, the latest in a line of hunters, gatherers, and conservationists who catalogue the anomalies and dangers that appear within Sturgeon, while making inroads with the nightmare and monster community looking to simply coexist. He proudly carries around the creature compendium, a family heirloom housing six generations of hard earned work. It is this success that led him to creating the Nightmare Detective agency where our story begins.

And, of course, there is no Sturgeon without its most famous warrior and, in her later years, mentor: Madame Nelle Lockwood. The woman our story centres around in her earliest days, long before she becomes the woman of fire, slayer of the bone spider scourge, and guide to the next cycle.

All cycles must have a beginning, and every threat must have its counterpart.

And so, I ask you to prime yourself for the coming storm. Settle yourself in for a tale of hardship, ugly conversations, violence, and intrigue.

Our view pans down from the darkened skies above, through great landmasses scorched by blackened fire and the steps of unseen colossal creatures out foraging, past the border separating the folklore from the mundane, through crowded streets and secret alleyways connecting various buildings until we reach a clearing and spy a lone towerhouse on a white marble street. A red and black gate surrounds the front garden, azaleas in full bloom and strange double-beaked birds fluttering gently around them. A sign hangs above the front door, the business name to where our story begins:

"Lockwood & McGraw: Nightmare Detective Agency."

The First Sin: Libidine (Lust)

Sin Eater: A person who consumes a ritual meal in order to spiritually take on the sins of a deceased person.

If only it were that simple.

My name is Eleanor Lockwood, but you can call me Nelle. I wouldn't call sin eating my job or anything superfluous like that—it's my reason for being.

My grandmother, Efa Lockwood, was one of the last in Wales to keep the practice going. With no mother or father to speak of, and no desire for children of my own, responsibility fell to me, the unlikely descendant, to take up the mantle and keep it going.

But I will be the last, that much is certain.

People have lost touch with that aspect of the world. The traditions of days gone by, respect for the old ways and the rituals that small towns and villages would undertake to safeguard their communities from wayward souls, unseen terrors, and creatures of the night.

When Efa met my grandfather Ajani, an immigrant from Jamaica, he brought with him stories of voodoo curses, known as Obeah. He taught of traditions held for centuries and the importance of respecting one's kin through practice. Things change swiftly though, and when I came of age, I knew I'd need to see the wider world to bring our family talents to prominence.

That's when I stumbled across Sturgeon. A town with a bar between places that caters to those in need, a town with a hotel sporting physical impossibilities on every floor, a town where the dead are ferried across on seaplanes, and where monsters meet martial artists in a tournament of nightmares.

But what I have to tell you all today goes far, far away from that—past the outer reaches of Sturgeon's eyes. We find ourselves situated in a maximum security prison in the middle of the most dangerous location on Earth:

The Bermuda Triangle.

I am The Last Sin Eater. And this is my story.

"Miss Lockwood, Mr. McGraw,

Your presence is urgently requested to deal with the final requests of our Death Row inmates. More information will be provided upon your acceptance and arrangements will be made to bring you here within forty-eight hours. Simply dial the number attached and we will organise the rest.
    I look forward to hearing from you.
    Yours faithfully,
    Warden Leichenberg."

Buck kicked back in his recliner and swirled his whiskey around lazily as I finished reading, smirking from underneath his Stetson.

"You gonna go? Hell, why am I even asking? O'course you are." He downed it in one and slammed the drink down as he gasped, standing up to his full height and cracking his back. He was a burly man in his early thirties, rippled muscles and a thick black beard hiding a chiselled brown jaw and piercing green eyes. Buck was as tough as they came, but calmer and more patient than most men twice his age. He never judged, never tried to speak for me, or tell me what to do. He respected me as an equal and I admired him all the more for it.

"Wonder what the hell kinda prison situates itself in the heart of a place like that, how do you even get in there without it being a crash and burn scenario?" I pondered aloud, taking note of the number and walking over to the landline in our office. We'd been operating as business partners for a couple of years, taking on odd jobs involving "unusual specimens and occurrences" that nobody else wanted. Buck called us "nightmare detectives." I called us scholars who were underpaid for our troubles.

"Makes sense to me, especially if the rumours of this place are true." Buck played with his beard and rifled through a book he'd picked from the large shelf on the back. "Tempestra Penitentiary is spoken of only in passing as a place where the most problematic individuals in history's shadows would be housed. Not your serial killers or political murderers, but the monsters that history tries its best to scrub from the pages. If we go, it's going to be a rough ride…" He snapped the book shut and grinned at me. My heart skipped a beat.

"Sounds like a hell of a hunt, I'm in."

One furtive phone call later and we were packed with our instructions to meet the porter at the airport.

"Caracossa Airways, you're sure about that, right?" Buck asked me, face buried in a notebook he'd been poring over in the weeks leading up to our letter from the warden. He called it his "greatest scholarly project," but never showed me a damn thing from it.

"Yep, they said a guy with a crow will greet us. Kinda hard to miss in Sturgeon, right? Even walking around with an Indiana Jones impersonator like you!" I chuckled, punching him in the arm playfully, my other hand running through the playlists on my iPod. I could never relax on a trip without some good music.

"Speak for yourself, you dress and act like you're trying your damnedest to be the next Van Helsing, albeit Welsh and female."

"And with better hair." I dramatically brushed a lock aside as we both laughed, the anxiety of a sea of people rushing past us ebbing away.

Out of the crowd came a tall man sporting all black attire and an over-excited crow on his shoulder, preening his hair and shouting, "BRAIN FOOD" as his owner tried and failed to coax him into calm.

"Damnit Edgar, I told you to cool it!" He hissed, offering up a finger for the corvid as a warning, instead making him tilt his head quizzically before nipping him and shrieking in delight.

"IT'S RAW! IT'S RAW!" He chirped as the man came closer, pinching his brow.

"You guys must be Lockwood and McGraw, could spot you two a mile away. Welcome to Caracossa Airways. I'm Nestor Holden and this little delight is Edgar; we'll be your guides to Tempestra Prison. You got everything you need? We won't be making any stops on the way. I've been instructed to assist in any way I can when we arrive, which is a pretty good excuse to get some R&R for us."

"RAW AND ROWDY! RAW AND ROWDY!" Edgar screeched as Nestor clicked in front of him. "What'd we say about crass behaviour in public?" He condemned.

"Only when funny." Edgar replied solemnly, his head lowered. Buck and I chuckled as we grabbed our bags.

"Oh, and by the way, I've been told to give you this before take off—keep it on you at all times. It's a charm to help ward off negative aura or something; my boss L. D. said it was imperative to get it to you."

He passed us each a totem. They were old and hand-carved, both sporting frail individuals whose bony hands held a thick hood in a perpetual state between up and down. It was impossible to tell if they were raising or lowering it. The figure's eyes were obscured.

It unsettled me, but I kept it in my pocket, as did Buck, and we departed.

For a split second as we passed through the terminal I spotted something in my peripheral vision: a thin, gangly sort of creature peering from behind a thin concrete beam that jutted out of the floor. Bioluminescent, black little eyes fixated on me and drool ran down its elongated lips, which curled into a smile as gnarled fingers awkwardly crunched until it was holding up a number in my direction. A number that would become synonymous with the rest of my life from that day forward.

The number seven.

The ride was interesting, to say the least. Our pilot was in a perpetual state of drunkenness, spouting off Lord Alfred Tennyson as he took us through rocky shores and across foreboding blackened skies. I had my music on and I'll be damned if it wasn't atmospheric when the opening riff kicked in.

As I looked out the window, Buck snoring something fierce next to me, my jaw fell slack at the sight that greeted me.

Where the ocean had been calm and the wind even more subdued for the duration of our journey, we were now greeted with a storm of tumultuous proportions. Sharp winds sliced at the window, whipping the ocean into a frenzy and slamming swathes of frothy green liquid at the plane with malice, trying in vain to stop us from approaching.

> *"The wrinkled sea beneath him crawls;*
> *He watches from his mountain walls,*
> *And like a thunderbolt he falls!"*

The pilot sang over the intercom as he took the plane into a nosedive, sending Buck's still snoring head forward with a snap. Edgar cried out as we descended further. My hands clasped the sides of the seat and my stomach was firmly in my boots.

"NO SURVIVORS! NO SURVIVORS!"

"Edgar! Don't mind him, we're fine. The approach is normal, for a place like this…" Nestor kept his arms crossed, seated opposite me in the flight attendant's area, eyes cast outside as bright lights began filling the windows. "Take a look. It's your new home for the next week."

Buck roused from his sleep just in time to catch a glimpse of the imposing structure awaiting us as the plane levelled out and we approached landing.

A circular structure spanning several thousand feet rose out of the sea. Torrents of water spilled off the top of the oval base and back into the ocean, leaving several landing pads visible as lights guided us in. At the centre of the structure was a thick steel tube that extended down into the depths.

All around the prison were heavy winds, crashing waves, and darkness for miles on end.

If someone wanted to escape, they'd find no respite upon getting out.

We were waved down by a sea of guards. A tall, imposing man stood in the back, outfitted in a black trench coat and a patterned umbrella sporting blue cherry blossoms. He waved dramatically as we stepped off the plane and a leather gloved hand clasped my own with extreme enthusiasm.

"Willkommen to my own personal tartarus! Do you like the location?" He beamed proudly at me, stretching his arms out and spinning around. "All of this just to prevent the worst of the worst from getting out. Crushing their hopes and dreams under mein steel-toe capped heel…" He turned back to us and Buck scoffed.

"Always the eccentric types in positions of power, huh?" he murmured, jabbing me playfully. "C'mon, indulge him. This *is* his kingdom, after all." With that, Buck strode forward, ignoring the rain and ocean froth drenching him in moments. He gave the warden a firm handshake before gesturing to me.

"Ah, you must be our revered sin eater! I've never seen what your people do up close and personal, but I will take great pride in seeing it enacted on our inmates, if it means they will suffer just a little bit more."

My eyebrow raised involuntarily. The warden noticed and immediately held his hands up defensively.

"Oh no, don't mistake me for a sadist! I just wish to ensure my job is done properly. These are bad, bad creatures. I deign to even call them people for what they've done. Each one has committed a crime... er, a 'sin' if you will, so egregious that God himself would sooner spit on his own son that allow a single one amongst them into the kingdom of Elysium."

"Are you a religious man, Mr. Leichenberg?" I asked, as Buck and I followed him to the central tube that connected the entrance to the main prison. Nestor and Edgar brought up the rear as the pilot cackled and took off again.

"Are you not, Madame Lockwood? In a world of such horrors as what we house here, one must have something to cling to that enables us to believe there is truth, justice, punishment, and reward. A balance for all things, such was the way the Greeks believed things to be. With your profession, I would've assumed you were a woman of the cloth, no?"

I shook my head as we piled into the chamber, the doors closing on our last look of the outside world for a week.

"If there is a God, he blinded himself to our struggles long ago. Whatever goes on here is up to us, now. I just do my part in the process."

Buck sighed and Nestor fed Edgar to keep him calm as we descended, the front section of the tube showing nothing but steel as we descended.

But after a moment, the view gave way to the top of a sprawling prison, the general population area. Thousands of inmates, some human and others... monsters in the literal sense. All clad in turquoise jumpsuits, they either congregated in groups doing jobs for the officers, or worked out. As we got closer, it became apparent this was a building far bigger and deeper than I could've imagined.

"Our prison houses seven thousand inmates of various backgrounds, crimes, and origins. We are tasked with making sure they never get out and cause more havoc up above. I'd inform you more of them or even give you a tour, but alas, we're not here for them..." The tube dropped down and we were plunged into darkness once more, save for a few maintenance lights that flooded the room in a red and purple hue.

"Your prison is expansive, Warden. I'm impressed. How many legendary beasts ya got locked up here? I'd enjoy cataloguing some of 'em for my compendium." Buck inquired.

The Warden seemed to think on it for a moment before politely shaking his head.

"Ah, my apologies, but there's no chance on your schedule. Each session will be difficult and take your day to complete. With seven of them, I do not wish to waste extra energy. But I am proud of the structure wherein these individuals are housed. Since my appointment to the position, we have had a far more complacent criminal populace and far less deaths!" He clapped his hands together excitedly as we came to a stop in front of a single white hallway.

"You know, I never envisioned getting my dream job by thirty-four, but here we are! Strange how the world works, no?"

He ushered us out and toward a makeshift office fitted with a bed, couch, vending machine, and research area.

"This is your workstation. We'll provide you with anything you may need and any extra facilities can be provided to you with an escort. Your first inmate is already waiting."

Placing my wet clothes and baggage down, I stared at him, incredulously.

"Now? What about any information on them first?"

A smile rippled across his face as his shoulders hunched. The man wasn't necessarily threatening, but his height coupled with the power he held here certainly made it an uncomfortable look.

"I want to see if your skills are as true as they come. His as well." He looked over at Buck who grinned back, but there was offence right behind it.

"What about me? I need a test?" Nestor quipped, Edgar trying to get at his eyebrows and preen them.

"No, you're a bodyguard. So long as you protect them, I think we have no issue. Even if I'm not fond of your... pet." Edgar cocked his head in the warden's direction before screeching:

"TASTY EYES! TASTY EYES!" Edgar laughed as Nestor scolded him.

"As good a time as any, I suppose. Let's go, lead the way, Warden."

With that, he escorted us out and down the long hallway, through the one locked door and out into a visitors centre of sorts. Several guards stood on watch and patted us down for contraband before we could even step foot into their interview areas.

"Welcome, Warden. Who are our esteemed guests today?"

"Cell two, Officer Mitchell. Prisoner #4822."

He passed us a pen to sign in with and nodded before buzzing the gate and allowing us through.

"Remember: if they catch you, we won't negotiate. Not for anything or anyone."

Nestor smiled as we went through to the interview room on the left of the cells.

"If I fail them, they're dead anyway."

The interview chamber was odd, to say the least. It was cordoned off from the rest of the building, as if quarantined. A small table with four chairs greeted us, a thick plexiglass window stretching across the length of the far wall, total darkness on the other side.

"The prisoner will be with you momentarily. I'll be watching from my office, but there is a button to the right of the wall if anything should go wrong. I'll speak with you after you're done. Good luck, Frau Lockwood!" He paused with the door held open, as if contemplating whether or not to say something else. "Don't be fooled by this one, looks can be… deceiving."

With that, the door shut and our first interview began.

For a moment, there was a silence that permeated the room, as if waiting for someone to start things off. Buck sat down with his compendium open and ready, a small microphone attached to a dictator machine. Nestor leaned against the wall and kept Edgar entertained.

I called out, hoping to get a response.

"The warden called you Prisoner #4822, but I'm hoping you have a more fitting name. Never been a fan of complexities. I'm

Madame Nelle Lockwood, the person you all asked to come here for your, uhh… sins. Are you there?"

Something shifted in the darkness. A thick, bulging, undulating shape that began wheezing and hacking as it moved forward.

"Yeah. I'm here, ma'am. Name's Tallulah Makepeace. Thank you for coming."

I felt something. Unsure what, I pressed on and tried to find a natural groove; the session wouldn't work if we didn't get off on a good footing.

"Why'd you ask for me? I understand none of you are particularly sorry for what you did." I may as well get the awkwardness out now, it seemed silly to ignore it. To her credit, she scoffed at my comment.

"Just because I ain't sorry, don't mean the sin shouldn't be excised. Maybe it'll make me feel remorse, who knows. I know what I did was wrong, but it was for a greater purpose. You'll see."

"You know what I do? How I do it?" I asked, the figure hacking and chuckling before replying.

"Yeah, I know whutchu do, honey. I got a lot of sins, but it's the early ones… the ones that put me in this metal coffin, that I needta get off my chest. And boy, if my chest ain't heavy enough already!"

She laughed and I began to get the impression she was a heavier woman, even with the shroud of darkness. Instead of pressing her to move forward, I did what I'd always done;

I encouraged her to tell her story.

"It all started when I was about eleven or twelve. I was a pretty young thang, lemme tell ya. Wore nice floral dresses, had fair skin, all the boys wanted to take me out. Heck, even the girls, not that I minded. Mama said I was her perfect angel. Problem was, I didn't care for any of 'em. Not really, anyway. They were just… there. Background noise to absorb when I needed attention, gifts, or favours. I tell ya, if the world had dropped another atom bomb and I was the only one left standin', I'm not sure I'd have been too concerned with the aftermath." She snorted and spat on the floor, clearing her throat before continuing.

"One night, right before Valentine's day, someone appeared at the end of my bed. He was tall, muscular, completely covered in red hair and washboard abs… I mean, my goodness…" She let out a shudder and I felt my skin crawl. "He said his name was Azazel and that he was an incubus, and someone had sent him here to pass on a message: I wasn't attaining my true form, but the form that others wanted me to partake. Until I became what he knew I could be, both inside and out, I was destined to be alone and unloved."

"So what did you do next, Tallulah? Were you inspired to change, or did you seek a doctor?" I asked, hands tapping the table as I gained a better idea of the woman in front of me.

"A doctor? Bitch, you crazy? I got a vision from my ideal man and he told me I had to change. You don't just ignore that. So, I did as I was told. Began eating more, not worrying about my hygiene unless my parents forced me to, but they gave up eventually. Stopped studying, dedicated myself wholeheartedly to the craft of perfection. Gained one hundred fifty pounds in just a few years, and my god… I was beautiful. I still am, o'course, but when you *see* yourself for the first time, it's like peeling off your old skin and steppin' out of a cocoon." She leaned back and I heard the chair groan under the pressure.

By now, a thick mist was forming around her. A byproduct of the session, but she wasn't to know just yet.

"Was it around this time you started luring young men and women into the woods, Tallulah?" Buck asked, his eyes dark and his grin replaced with a scowl.

"You must've been around seventeen when you started, right? I know the name and what you did."

Tallulah shifted in her seat and made an approving noise, leaning in the darkness to see Buck better.

"My, my. As if it weren't enough to have one looker in here, I got two. Are y'all helping me with a sin to be eaten or are y'all the snacks? You look good enough to eat." She giggled and continued. "When I completed the physical metamorphosis, Azazel came back to me, cooing in my ear that to have the perfect love, I had to be willing to give up everything and go further. To take love from others."

She scratched at her face, thick calluses resisting the nails. I swear I heard a pimple pop. My stomach turned but I ignored the desire to lose composure.

"The first few, I just told 'em there was an animal in need or that I'd lost my baby brother in the woods. I guess the damsel in distress thang is still pretty popular. They'd always come in, help me, and get caught... that's where the real process began. See, it weren't enough to just kill 'em. The point of true love was to carry them with you forever. To take their lives, take a piece of 'em and ensure it was always a part of ya. *That* was true power." She leaned forward, and it took every inch of my body not to recoil in horror.

She was a gargantuan woman in her thirties, and easily six hundred pounds. Undulating fat and heavy folds spilled out of her turquoise jumpsuit and over the chair. Her black hair was matted to her head and her facial features were so sunken into her elongated and fattened skull that I struggled to comprehend how she saw anything. But that mouth... my god, it was double the size of my own. The teeth were yellowed and the gums bright red. Random hairs and pimples littered her face like badges of honour.

"See, they say bees make the best honey, but that ain't quite true. Azazel taught me all about the mummification of old human beings. Men and women who willingly gave their bodies to be something more. But there are far quicker ways to make it happen if you have a guiding voice."

She grinned and a long, black tongue escaped her lips, like a serpent tasting the air around a frightened victim.

"I'd make sure the holes were deep; the coffins were done perfectly to their measurements. It helped to have a friendly neighbour who made 'em special for me if I gave him... favours, in return. Once they fell in, the drop was steep enough that they couldn't get back out. The liquid would act like a gelling agent, stoppin' em from going very far until I came back with the rest of the ingredients. Watchin' 'em struggle like flies in a trap was always immensely satisfying."

She groaned and the hairs on my body stood on end. It felt more and more like I was being sized up. The red and pink mist filling her room was now gaining mass at a rapid rate.

"So you made these people into food?" I asked, trying not to dry heave as I finished my sentence.

"Mhmm. They'd struggle until their strength gave out and their heads fell under the water. Then, I'd put the lid on and wait. My own little Garden of Eden... it was like I was a god in my own

The Last Sin Eater

backyard. Give it just two months, they'd be nothin' more than a sweet liquid that kept me young, beautiful, and immortal. So long as I had that sweet nectar, I weren't goin' nowhere. I had a task to fulfill and a part to play, so sayeth Azazel. I couldn't stop until I met the one I was destined to fall in love with."

"But that's not all you did, is it? Because if it was, we'd be done by now." I pressed on. The mist began to form into a shape, but wasn't quite there. Tallulah shifted uncomfortably in her seat, finally showing a degree of emotion before she continued.

"I started to lose track of how many I was putting into the pits. Didn't matter if it were a couple, an older guy, a younger girl. Whatever. I knew to be smart and to be careful. Never any personal ties. So, when Candace wandered in…" She paused, beady little eyes welling up with tears and her jowls quivering with sadness. "I broke my only rule. My little girl was only three when she went out to play. She wandered into an open pit that I'd dug for our next victim. He was a playmate of hers and if she'd just… just waited a little bit longer…"

She burst into tears, greasy, filthy hands covering her face as she sobbed heavily.

"And after that, you gave yourself up?" It seemed too convenient, but she nodded, snot running down her face.

"I saw no way forward with mine or Azazel's goal without Candace. My progeny. So, I gave myself up and here I am. Waitin' for death."

The haze was nearly fully formed now, but something was still missing.

"That's not the worst of it, is it, Tallulah?" Buck pressed, something in his voice commanding the room. "You lured people in with pity and sexual favours, we're expected to believe you had a soft spot? I don't buy it. I know what the greatest sacrifices entail. Candace didn't wander in there, did she?"

The crying grew louder as Buck pressed her more.

It took a moment, but her demeanour shifted once again. I have never felt more like a diver in a shark tank waiting to be devoured. Every fibre of my being urged me to run as the crying gave way to uproarious laughter and a thunderous pounding against the plexiglass, damn near causing me to jump out of my skin as she cackled.

"Aw, I thought my actin' would've fooled y'all! Guess I'm losin' my charm, huh?"

I felt sick, my nostrils filling with the scent of honey. I knew we were close.

"Naw, I didn't give myself up outta grief. I did it because Candace was the last one. My little angel with her pink bow, flowing locks and curly hair, she saw me as a god... but I saw her as a means to an end. A love unrequited from daughter to mother. She didn't even put up a fight when I dropped her into the pit. Just looked up at me with those doe eyes and said 'Mama, why?' as I poured the mixture in. And lemme tell ya..."

Tallulah leaned forward, her fetid breath fogging up the glass as the mist around her took the shape of a tall man with thick horns, clad in red fur. Yellow eyes beamed at Tallulah with an expectant grin as she resumed speaking.

"She was the most delicious of 'em all. And they're with me always. All of 'em."

"Tallulah, why even have me here if you've got no real fears of what happens next? Why put us through that sordid and disgusting tale?" I tried to keep my emotions in check, struggling to hold my nerve.

"Because I wanted someone to look at my beauty one last time and see me, unburdened by sin, as I move to the next phase. This is just the first part, you were my witness. That's all there is to it."

She got out of her seat as I held back my sheer disgust, knowing in a few moments I'd need to devour the sin. She cracked her large back and neck, smiling at us as if we were those same victims she'd lured into the woods, moments away from their death.

"Been nice meetin' ya, glad you were there to hear my sin. But, time's a wastin'. Azazel and I are off to greener pastures of godhood. I'm sure we'll see one another again, someday."

With that, she walked over to the man, and embraced him in a passionate kiss as he pinched her nose with one hand, gripping her throat with the other. She struggled and despite her sheer weight and height advantage, could not break his grip. I watched in horror as her fighting grew weaker. As her arms became limp, he pulled away to crack her neck and let her fall to the floor.

His eyes scanned us once before Buck called his name and he faded from the room in a puff of smoke.

Nestor ran for the panic button and pushed it as the sirens rang out and furtive footsteps rushed down the hall.

I was already fixated on the final part of the ritual.

Some sin eaters only needed to devour the sin in a meal form, carrying it with them and moving on. But in my case, there had to be a story, a reason and connection. Now, I'm staring down the end result of this creature's exploits, knowing it will be a part of me forevermore.

In front of me lay a small bowl filled with a golden liquid that bubbled and frothed. I knew I had to eat it, to finish the ritual, but there was something stopping me. Something I could see in the broth that made me realise I would regret visiting this prison for the rest of my life.

A lock of hair, tied with a small pink bow, floating on the surface before fizzling away.

Eyes closed and hands trembling, I brought the bowl to my lips and did as I was instructed to.

I devoured the sin.

Inmate #4822: *Tallulah Makepeace*
Sin: *Lust*
Food: *Mellified Man.*

The Second Sin: Avaritia (Greed)

In the moments following our tumultuous affair with Tallulah, the woman representing "lust," I forced down the broth of mellified man and felt my entire body caked in that sickly sensation you get after downing cod liver oil. It made every facet of my being wretch and try its damnedest to pull the liquid back up from my stomach.

But any good sin eater worth their training knows better than to ruin a good ritual.

Buck saw me struggling and took my hand as the guards funnelled in, rushing onto both sides of the plexiglass, one group to check on us and the other to hoist the gargantuan form of Tallulah off of the floor and onto a makeshift stretcher. It was obvious even from here that it wouldn't be enough to hold her frame.

"Hey, Nellie. Look at me." He spoke softly, and I felt the bile rise in my stomach, but did as he told me. I stared at him for what felt like minutes. His calm demeanour put me at ease. The acid in my chest fought to stay up but rapidly dissipated as he put his hands on my shoulders and kissed my forehead. When he pulled away, his breath was hot, and he looked pained, but settled down quickly.

"Any time you get like that, you just lean on me, okay? I'm your safeguard. That's what I'm here for. Well..." he side-eyed the compendium on the desk, the page flipped open to a news report about "The Mellified Woman of Utah" and turned back, a sly grin on his face that made me melt. "That and building on this ol' book. Mama McGraw won't be happy if I don't complete it soon!"

I got up and gazed over at the book. His mother was the matriarch of the McGraw clan, an old and powerful group of cryptozoologists who for centuries had protected the shores of the UK from threats both outside and inside the nation, from creatures older than any structure, more powerful than any king, and wiser than any elder. Buck's job was to ensure that all was catalogued, and the pages filled, before his ascension to the elder status.

I wonder if he knew what that book would come to be. What it would represent.

The guards escorted us out and an expectant warden stood between us and the break room, his hands outstretched and his smile wide.

"Wunderbar! You did excellently, mein devourer of sins! I was most impressed, though a little surprised with the aftermath… did you intend to have such an encounter?"

"No. I never know how these things will occur when I start. I simply let the conversation flow and like a breeze in the sails, carry me to wherever it leads. But, right now, I just wanna sleep. I'd have appreciated knowing who she was before I went in there. What I'd need to consume."

If the warden recognised my not-so-subtle plea to move, he ignored it with expertise.

"Now, you have some twelve hours until your next appointment with Prisoner #6572, but I must warn you, this one's tale is more unpleasant than the last. They're young, but do not mistake that youth for naivete. They make Prisoner #4822 seem tame in comparison."

"Why do I feel like you're gonna say that for every interview we have?" Buck's eyes narrowed and Edgar croaked away, flapping his wings as the warden paced near him.

"CORPSE HOARDER. CORPSE HOARDER. FLEE."

The warden looked closely at him before smiling wide, the warmth returning to his jubilant face.

"Because I will. This is not an easy task, and I would be wasting a most valuable resource if I sent you to the wolves right off the bat. Instead, you are going with what I feel is the most appropriate difficulty curve. That just so happens to be #6752. I'll forward you some papers to look over, but I would prefer if only you and the bird man knew the information. The less the sin eater knows, the better."

"Why? Think I can't handle it? *You* called *me* here, Warden Leichenberg." I spat. I was tired and now insulted. He shook his head and sighed.

"It is because you clearly empathise too much. A sin eater carries the burdens of their sinner for all time. I wish to see you live through this, not be crushed by it. You *are* the last sin eater, we must be mindful of that. Besides, what kind of warden would ein be if I let a guest die in my prison?"

With that, he clicked his fingers, and the men followed at his heels, pushing the partially obscured body of Tallulah along the hall and out of sight. We filed into the break room and I collapsed in a heap onto the bed, exhaustion taking me over.

Between the trip and the thoughts of what she had done, my entire body was wracked with fatigue. I hadn't been this worn out since my first sin eating session ten years prior.

Drifting in and out of sleep, I heard the muffled voices of Buck, Nestor, and occasionally Edgar discussing the papers in front of them. Their voices were steeped in disgust, concern, and anxious strategies. I heard them pinning things to the board and keywords like "stitched," "malformed," and "freak," but nothing more as deep sleep took me.

It was there I had my recurring dream. The night I was taken from my home and put into the care of my grandparents.

The night I realised I was a sin eater.

Mum had cooked a pot roast and was watching a nature programme with David Attenborough. I loved his voice, still do. His soothing cadences and love of nature resonated with a young me, who spent her time cataloguing bugs in the back garden and dreaming of one day going on grand adventures to find untold secrets and creatures.

I remember looking out on our driveway, toward the main road which bordered on the new forest. Mum was a forest ranger and routinely had to go out for calls. Sometimes there would be an animal incident where a deer ran into a car, other times there could be a small forest fire, or some dickhead teenagers setting off fireworks.

This time was different. Her voice was panicked, and she grabbed her keys, telling me to lock up and not touch the oven as she'd be back in thirty minutes.

There's a gap after this. There always is. But I recall the purple glow from the clearing, the loud booming sound, and the searing hot pain filling my lungs.

Then, I would see a face leering over me, upside down and features contorted as it leaned closer, before waking up in a cold sweat.

But this time, I saw something new. That creature from the airport. Features even more horrifying as they pressed up close to my own, the smell of its sin overbearing my nose and making my eyes water.

The smell of a rotting corpse.

It smiled and held out those gnarled fingers again, this time dropping one digit slowly into its grotesque fist to reveal a number:

Six.

Waking up, the lights were dimmed and Buck was nowhere to be seen, nor was his book. Nestor sat in the seat facing opposite, keeping a watchful eye while cradling a sleeping Edgar. When he wasn't screeching out expletives or being a smartass, he was downright adorable. A small black fuzzy baby at peace in his arms.

"You know I found him the day I lost everything? I stood amid the smoulders of my home and found a small black egg that I assumed was seared from the flames. But no, it was just that. An obsidian egg, untouched by the surrounding destruction. I felt a desire to protect him, especially considering I couldn't protect them. He bonded with me immediately and picked up words far quicker than any corvid should. Hell, sometimes I think he was brought to me by Lady Death, but that'd be too convenient." He stroked Edgar's feathers softly as he made faint cooing sounds.

"I trust you know my sin, Nelle?" He asked, breaking the silence and adding a weight to the room. He was smiling, but the guilt hung over him like a deluge of emotional weight.

"Yeah. Lesser wrath. You made a bad call, and it cost you everything. Your partner, your two boys, your livelihood. Lady Death made a deal, and here you are. Your sin is in several small parts that cling to you wherever you roam. They smell of sulphur and brimstone, but taste of apples and tears." I got up and walked to him, kneeling in front of his tired face, and took his hands in mine. "You are not a bad person, Nestor. I don't sense it, and neither does Buck. You are a protector. If you've got my back, I've got yours."

Edgar stirred in his arms and mumbled, "Papa. Safety. Papa. Love." before ruffling his feathers. Nestor's eyes glazed over and he sniffed, nodding with thanks as I stretched and made myself something to eat, desperate to get the taste of honey out of my mouth.

"Do you think the next sin will really be as bad as the warden claims?" He asked, looking up at the clock. Three hours to go until we were due to interview them.

"I think if the Warden wanted to lie to us, he'd try something a bit more complex. So yeah, I'm not ruling anything out." I sighed and took a long sip from my chamomile tea, the aroma helping to eradicate mellified man, my tastebuds grateful as it passed my tongue.

"But you gotta think, a guy with the name 'corpses on a mountain' isn't to be trusted."

—

We sat and waited for the prisoner, having followed the same procedures as before. This time, a sense of anticipation and dread hung in the air. Not only because of how the last one had gone, but because both Nestor and Buck knew something I didn't. Something they desperately wanted to reveal from under the watchful eye of the warden.

And it was killing them to hide it.

I rolled up my sleeves, took a deep breath in, and listened— the sound of someone being wheeled in from the other side of the plexiglass. Unlike the gurney our previous inmate was removed on, this was a wheelchair with restraints. The person sat hidden behind the low lighting once more.

"May I ask your name before we begin? It's more informal in comparison to your assigned number."

The form cocked its head to the side and held up its hand in a conversational form, whispering to it before responding to us.

"Names are powerful things. For now, you may address us as Emarosa. We contain all things beautiful." They leaned forward, wiry brown hair poking through the shadows and giving us a glimpse at the owner. "And you are our sin eater. Most good. We have a sin that we want excised from us. It is the one thing we do not want."

"Very well, that's what I'm here for, Emarosa. Tell me how your sin came to be. What formed it?"

"We realised early on that we craved more than our means provided. Birth givers did their best with meagre offerings, passing fancies and trinkets that ultimately meant nothing to us. We sought greater things, lesser things. All things. But we were young, weak, and unable to do such things on our own. We listened and waited until we matured enough to progress."

"Listened? To whom?" I pressed, their third person schtick already wearing on me, even if it was fascinating. They leaned back in the chair, their body shaking with excitement.

"Our saviour. One of our guiding lights: Moloch."

The room rumbled. A soft heat flowed in from the corners and I saw the red haze begin permeating around the back of Emarosa's chair.

"The Canaanite god? That Moloch?" Buck scanned his book, putting a finger on the article and sliding it toward me. Depictions of children thrown into the monstrosity's belly, screaming and reaching out for despondent parents as they're cast into the flames, the god's nose billowing smoke. I felt sick.

"Yes. Though he did not request such acts in his name. He came to us in a dream on our eighteenth birthday, informing us we were a vessel for him to inhabit one day. But in order to do so, we had to take from everyone else around us. We had to expand our horizons and our skills. So, we set off to be a doctor and learn the tools of the trade. It was imperative for our metamorphosis. I trust when you spoke to Makepeace, she informed you of something similar?"

I recalled her discussion over growing larger, less clean, and eschewing hygiene. Ignoring the desire to shiver, I nodded.

"We had a similar one. Do you not think that it is right for people to grow and change? To desire more than their position offers? Perhaps to aspire for greater things, things that others have. We do not think it such a strange concept—people take from others all the time in order to survive."

Buck interjected as Nestor stared daggers at Emarosa.

"That ain't what you did though, is it? You didn't just take to survive. In fact, you never took to survive. You simply ransacked. A thief in the lowest sense of the word." His fists clenched and his teeth gritted. I held up a hand to stop him.

"It's all right, we're fine. I promise." Before he could protest, I put on my firmest voice to ensure I didn't lose Emarosa's respect. "Not another word."

He sat back, shoulders falling under the weight of his words, and focused instead on the compendium and the haze.

"Organs count as vital survival items, you know. We simply required more of them than the usual person." Emarosa quipped, and for the first time, I sensed something other than neutrality in their tone.

"I need you to sit forward so I can see you, Emarosa. I don't believe we can conduct this properly if you are hidden."

There was a murmuring as the form shifted. Another voice spoke, this one gruff and masculine, sounding like they'd swallowed an ashtray and washed it down with bourbon.

"The fuck is this? You think you can take from *me*? I. Own. You. I own all of this. I do what I want because the money in my bank account and the status I covet makes it so. Fuck you. I ain't moving for shit!"

I was taken aback. This was coming out of nowhere and it certainly didn't match the aloof tone they'd displayed before. What was this?

"To whom am I speaking now?" I asked, trying to get a handle on the situation, but the form shifted again, becoming elegant, draping one leg over the other, hands folded on their knee.

"Oh, dear. You feel you have the status to address *me*? I'm a queen in my own home and I do not speak to the lowly dregs such as you. I can buy and sell you in the blink of an eye, bitch."

The form argued with itself until settling down and shaking its head. It sighed and leaned forward into the light, displaying its true horror.

It took everything in me not to scream.

Modern day Prometheus. It was the only thing that came to mind at that moment as the haze split off into two patterns on the sides of their containment chamber. The hair was wiry on one side, slicked back on the other. The head was filled with stitched and sutured segments of discoloured flesh, extra eyes drooping in places they shouldn't be, two distinct faces leering at us as several smaller pain-addled faces on their neck and cheeks groaned in protest. One barely masculine face to the left and a slightly more feminine to the right, one all-encompassing mouth at the centre. Thick black lips, revealing innumerable teeth, parted for speech.

They were an amalgamation of other human beings. Even when they spoke, the tongue was forked and split into two directions.

"We were once two. Our names no longer matter to anyone but you, it seems. Donnel and Millicent Cartwright. We knew our callings were unique, but we had no idea that there would be two. One for each greedy twin. Where Donnel had Moloch crooning in their ear, Millicent heard from Mammon, the represcenter of ill-gotten wealth. Though, to us, any wealth acquired by our form meant it was always ours. Alas, we wanted more…"

Buck scanned a newspaper article, but wouldn't show it to me. I could make out the words "organ thief," and my suspicions were confirmed. The mists were almost complete.

"Why did you steal people's identities? Why take from them in this way? I know greed to be about food, money, power—but why this?"

Emarosa pondered for a moment, both faces looking to each other before responding.

"The greatest power is that of domination of the soul. Own a person's flesh, own their entire being. Mammon and Moloch had different ways of saying such things to us, but we knew that in order for us to ascend to the next level, we had to acquire a set amount of souls. Our greed would need to be tested." They stopped for a moment, hesitant.

"We would need to be tested before we came in front of you. The greediest woman of all time in equally avaricious company."

I felt the hot flash of anger rise in me at that statement. To be called such a thing by a monstrous killer was infuriating. I worked to maintain my composure as Nestor and Edgar leaned forward, perhaps expecting trouble.

"I consume sins to absolve the person, to set them free. That does *not* make me greedy, nor are Buck and Nestor." I breathed deeply, trying to keep things on track. "You're leading up to the sin you wish to tell; what is it?"

But Emarosa was not done. They tapped their heads with a spindly finger in tandem.

"But you carry all those sins. Such a beautiful method for absorbing others that we could never wish to acquire. Mr. McGraw is attempting to acquire all the knowledge on beasts and people like us for his own self gain. Mr. Holden over there lost everything through greed and still wants more." They smiled, those white pillars shimmering from their jaws. "I am fed as much information as I wish. We are not so different."

"The sin, if you could. I am a busy woman." I replied curtly. I didn't like my own character being brought into question. Nestor and Buck both held their nerve as best they could.

The soft, feminine voice returned.

"I began acquiring the souls necessary for ascension. It was not easy work, but my brother and I are remarkably efficient with our hands. We would make sure the subject was someone who had something we wanted. It started out as money, food, status. A reason to justify our cause, in those earlier days…"

Donnel butted in.

"But, you eventually realise that it doesn't matter. None of it matters. It was our destiny to take, and take we did. Every single one served a greater purpose, stitched into our fabric and becoming a part of us. Burning what we didn't need in service to Lord Moloch."

"And Lord Mammon, yes." Millicent remarked, her voice quivering with emotion. "But we knew there would be a greater sacrifice needed. Especially upon our eighteenth birthday, as our loving family discovered our secret. One of our playthings had woken up and managed to escape from the basement. Before Papa could even question it, Donnel bludgeoned him to death. I set upon Mother and used the boiling water from the stove to burn her flesh and cave her soft skull in with a frying pan."

The mists were almost complete, the shapes of a large bull with the legs of a man and the tail of a scorpion on the left, a heavyset man with a golden crown and a slew of jewelry, his gut exposed, and a smile crossing his wide face on the right.

"We made sure the siblings didn't suffer much. But we were pressed for time, and both voices rang in our ears. We could not stand to be apart from the family or each other. So, with what time we had, we put our skills to the test one last time."

Food had begun filling up my table. Plates upon plates of meat cooked to perfection stacked themselves in front of me. The aroma of bacon and eggs filled the air. I was not hungry.

"They screamed so much that our ears bled. We worked diligently to scrap them as best we could before bringing them into ourselves and joining us together in the beautiful form you see here. Emarosa is the nirvana state we hoped to reach before we met with you, our god of greed."

As the mists filled, Emarosa rose from their seat on extremely fragile legs, four knees threatening to buckle as this towering mass of flesh and limbs took tentative steps toward the plexiglass, placing one hand against it. Those hands had strangled, cut, ripped and torn apart innocent people. They'd harvested their organs, their bones, their flesh. Taking what they wanted.

Those truly were the hands of greed.

"Our sole regret is that we couldn't take more of them, as is our birthright. We were instructed to tell our deeds and lay our sins bare. That we have done. Now, we move to the final stage of consumption."

They took their hand away as the meat continued to pile, Nestor stepping forward to stop it tumbling over. I shook my head. This was the final moment.

"This ascension… what is it? What does it mean?" I knew this may be my last chance to ask them. I was already becoming eerily familiar with what the end brought these interviews.

They smiled as the heads displayed individual expressions of joy.

"It means we will consume everything. Not a single shard of light will be out of our grasp. So it is written. Good luck, my lady. You will need it for the road ahead. I can't imagine how hard it will be for someone as greedy as you to sacrifice anything, but you will need to before this task is complete."

As the mist finished, both figures walked toward Emarosa, somehow towering over even them.

Moloch put a pair of huge anvil-like fists on Donnel's face, as Mammon placed bright red, muscled hands upon Millicent's.

Then, without warning, they pulled.

The screaming was unholy, each face and patchwork person shrieking at the top of their lungs, but neither one relented. Slowly, the skin separated from the body and partially intact people were pulled away into their corners. The remains of Emarosa collapsed to the floor with a sickening wet squelch.

Donnel was pushed into the open, fiery belly of Moloch, his screams rippling and echoing as his red eyes gleamed.

Millicent was put on her knees in front of Mammon, who opened his monstrously large jaws. He picked her up by her waist and forcibly bit down on the top half of her, a spurt of blood staining the plexiglass as he continued to devour the rest of her, kicking in protest—and perhaps even joy.

Buck and Nestor sprung forward to stop me, but I knew I had to eat the food. The ritual was useless without it. I closed my eyes and took a bite, the surrounding commotion largely blocked out.

The first bite was soft. Some blood dribbled out and stained my chin. The meat was tender and melted in my mouth as it began to run down my throat. After the mellified man, this was ambrosia. I began biting down harder, consuming more voraciously, trying to clear my plate as quick as I could, my stomach expanding to accommodate the extra contents… yet I never felt full or even remotely bloated. It was as though the food was simply evaporating when I swallowed. I was enjoying it, but only after I gave pause to breathe did I realise that not only was this not true food, but I was choking. Tough, coarse meat filled my throat and burned my nostrils. Thick, unyielding fat was staining my teeth and entrenching itself in my throat, filling my sinuses and making my eyes water.

The taste was horrifying—but not as much as the feeling of thumping in my throat as I pushed hard to swallow. It resisted and felt like it was a small egg I'd elected to attempt eating in one go. I swear I felt it push against me as my body writhed and desperately tried to push it down. I was determined to finish, I couldn't fail here.

It was only when Buck pulled me away and Edgar swooped down to stare at me, crowing "MEAT. MEAT. TASTY MEAT." that I realised what was going on.

The plate of meat wasn't steaks. It wasn't chicken or anything even close. As Buck thumped my back in an effort to help me throw it up, I instead swallowed and felt something iron-tasting fall into my stomach.

What lay left on the plate was a single human heart, still beating faintly. A small congealed pool of blood lay around it.

I'd just eaten what remained of the entire family.

Inmate #6572: *Donnel and Millicent Cartwright, known collectively as "Emarosa."*
Sin: *Greed*
Food: *Steak…The Cartwright Family.*

The Third Sin: Invidia (Envy)

To say it's been a rough forty-eight hours would be a gross understatement, and I do mean gross.

My body did not react to the food very well. As I stared down at the now empty plate, my world grew hazy and my body became limp as toxic shock overcame me.

For a while, I simply floated in the stygian void between worlds. I saw very little save for flashes of bioluminescent colours, beautiful patterns that raced past my eyes and bore into my skull, pushing the endorphins out to my aching limbs. I could hear voices off in the distance, but I was so high above it all that it mattered little.

As I concentrated, shapes would convalesce and form out of the dredges of darkness. Bountiful planets, beauteous stars, and stellar galaxies that appeared far closer than they actually were, each individual strand of its great cosmic arms winking at me in morse code. A greeting? No, a warning.

"S. O. S."

Something else formed on the fringe of my peripheral vision, a vacuous black hole with an event horizon that spanned the stretch of my view. It was a bright orange hue with a thick, pungent red that pulsated as the hole grew larger, devouring anything that came near it with great expediency.

Then, out of its murky depths, a long arm punctured the blackness, colossal and pulling itself free as a body began to emerge.

The same spectre that's plagued me since before I got onto the plane here. It unhinged its jaws and began biting down on a nearby planet, ripping it to pieces with razor teeth and staining its mouth as if the planet were a ripe fruit.

Stretching out its gnarled fingers once more, it clenched a fist around the planet. It held up five fingers with the free hand, the other firmly shut on the crumbled planet as it cackled in such a wicked way that it snapped me from my sleep.

"Five."

The first thing I felt when I awoke was a pounding sensation in my head. Mainly because as I snapped awake and stood up, my skull collided with the warden's in a sickening thud.

"Ach! Mein gott woman, I was just inspecting you to ensure there was no lasting damage!" He stumbled back, clutching his forehead as I did my own. Nestor rushed in and looked ready for a fight before seeing the state we were in.

"Nelle! You good? You've been out for a day and a half; we were getting worried. Warden here said he'd have to pull the plug if you didn't get up soon."

The warden shifted uncomfortably before looking over at me, his lips curling into a half smile as he shrugged playfully.

"What matters now, mein fraulein, is that you're awake and ready for your next sin. Emarosa was a unique challenge, but one I was confident you could overcome—even if the food was regrettable." He shivered as our minds were cast back to the plate of meat. Cartwright family meat.

"Not your fault. Nobody knows what the food will be until it happens. But no more games from this point on, okay? I want to know what I'm dealing with when I walk in there. Especially after this latest scare." I stood up and walked toward him, a finger outstretched in an accusatory manner, trying my best to be intimidating against a tall man whose name literally translated to 'corpse mountain.' "Am I clear?"

For a split second, I thought he would do something drastic—strike me where I stood or spit in my face. His expression was nothing short of utter incredulity that someone spoke to him this way. In an instant, it snapped back to the wild eccentricity he'd shown throughout, and he nodded exuberantly.

"Ja, Ja. I think you proved you can handle it. Very well. Our next inmate is Prisoner #2122, Ethan Elliot Blaznik III, a twenty-two-year-old programmer who committed a series of kidnappings and torture killings on young men and women in the Washington area. His sin is his own to tell, but I should caution you: this man will use his information against you and try to get a rise out of you. Why? I cannot say. But he has made… comments about you in his summons. I suspect he has reasons for you being here beyond the request."

The warden went for the door, informing us we had four hours to prep.

Glancing around the room for anything non-meat related, my eyes stumbled over the open compendium. It sat on a photo of Buck and his entire family. He was younger, his famous beard little more than a stubble on his chiselled jaw, and sporting a more conservative explorers outfit than the one he proudly wears now. Around his sides are two elder brothers, Darius and Johnny, his sister Tara, and cousins Porter, Solomon, and Brandon. His father Nathaniel stood proudly by him, huge hands resting gently on his shoulders. His wife, Buck's mother Saoirse, lovingly nestled in his chest, beaming down at her boy. In front of them all on this proud occasion was the hunting trophy that Buck had claimed as a rite of passage; he'd successfully taken down a wayward lycanthrope with nothing but his wit and a bowie knife.

Buck hated killing anything without cause, but this was one creature he couldn't ignore even then. It'd been devouring children who ventured too far from the safety of the village and venturing into forest territory where this intelligent killer would wait. They say when Buck sliced its stomach open, two children spilled out—neither alive, sadly. It was here that Buck got his nickname, holding onto the beast as it thrashed around and tried desperately to free itself from his grip, bucking him around as he drove the knife into its ears and eyes repeatedly. Simon would forever cease to be his first name henceforth. "Buck Nasty McGraw" was born on that day.

I smiled, the photo bringing such warmth and comfort after a physically exhausting few days. I traced my hands over it, remembering the good times when we'd first met.

"Hard to believe it was ten years ago already, ain't it?" Buck called, passing me a hot drink and sitting next to me as I observed the photo with wistful eyes. "I met you on the very first job I took as a licensed crypto-hunter and cataloguer. You were still in training then with your grandparents, must've been a few days shy of sixteen when you assisted me in taking down that elusive forest god. You talked to him for what felt like hours to get his sin while I tried to subdue him."

"And then he reared back, bleated, and ran headfirst into a tree, knocking you both out cold. Yes, I remember." I chuckled, his eyes rolling at the mere mention of his failure as he began laughing.

"How was I to know he was more goat than god? Still, that was the day I was given one of the most important life lessons I'd carry into our working relationship all these years later."

I looked at the note left at the bottom of the photo, the one that Buck coveted like it was the most valuable piece of treasure he'd ever owned or would own.

"*Son,*

Today, you are my equal. Tomorrow, you will surpass that.
The compendium is now your responsibility and your job to fill.
But promise me, son, you won't forget the family and will embody our most important trait.
Make as many connections along the way as you can, for our time is fleeting and all cycles must one day repeat.
With all the love in the world,
Dad"

"What lesson might that be, Buck?" I asked, smiling as he took my hands in his and those hazel eyes shone with pride and admiration.

"That Nelle Lockwood is stronger than I could ever hope to be, and if she can talk a forest god into stupidity, she can beat any sinner or monstrosity this world has to throw at her. And I will support her every goddamn step of the way. I did it when we hit the coma city, I did it when we dealt with the dreamwalker, and I will do it until my dying breath."

I felt weak, partially from the sentiment, as well as the lack of actual food over a day and a half. I nodded affirmatively, and he patted my hands before fixing me something to eat after hearing my stomach groan in protest.

"We're also here, y'know, if you need anything fucking up. That's our whole modus operandi."

"RIP AND TEAR. RIP AND TEAR." Edgar chimed in, mocking Nestor's "Stop it!" as he tried to silence him, bringing an even bigger smile to my face.

In spite of where I was and how I felt, I was truly blessed.

Even if the image of that fucking creature in my dreams still loomed on the edges of my vision.

When the announcement rang out for us to go toward the visitation area, there was a sense of concern amongst us all that things were going to reach a critical mass point that we would be completely and utterly unable to bounce back from. I know in my case, the pervasive question that lingered in my mind was simple:

How many of these sins could I take before they began to consume every good part of me?

I kept close to the others and tried to keep my mind focused on the job at hand, not the mounting list of concerns I had about this facility, the inhabitants, or my own competency. As we passed the gate, I heard soft music coming from the interview room.

"Is that normal?" I asked the guard. He kept his gaze firmly on the door handle as he scanned his ID card and waited for the green light.

"For most? No. But for the death row inmates, yes. Some you've seen already don't care for furnishing these little spaces, but Blaznik and the others do. If the music is ever too loud, just get Holden to come out and we'll instruct him to turn it down. Oh, and uhh… try to keep calm in there. He has a habit of riling people up."

The machine beeped, and the door swung open to let loose the hard EDM blasting from the inmate's side. Strobe lighting beamed across the room, revealing a young man. He was short in stature, muscular on the top half of his frame, the bottom half remarkably skinny and without definition. He was throwing his entire weight behind his arms as he danced around the room, smashing anything in his wake and frequently hitting the same spot on the wall with extreme ferocity. His knuckles bashed into concrete as he screeched at the top of his lungs. Something meshed in with the wall, blood and skin on his fists as he pulled away, breathing heavily as the song came to an end.

The Last Sin Eater

It was a photo of someone. The image was faded and crumpled, but the smile of a charming young woman in her late teens or early twenties still shined through.

"You're Ethan, right? I'm Nel—"

Before I could finish, he held up a bloodied knuckle and extended his index finger toward me, wagging it as we took our seats.

"No. That is not how this works, my dear. You will address me by my *full* title and only then will I respond." He breathed in, hunching his shoulders and flexing. "Bitches really think they're so entitled, don't they?"

I felt anger surge through me. I didn't take to insults or a lack of respect at the best of times, but I knew better than to let advice given to me just moments ago fly out the window. I pulled up my chair and closed my eyes for a moment before responding.

"My apologies. Mr. Ethan Elliot Blaznik III, my name is Miss Nelle Lockwood. My associates are—"

Again, he wagged his finger as he pulled out a beanbag chair, undamaged from the tantrum moments ago and sank into it. His legs were splayed out and he attempted to keep the bulge within his sweatpants visible at all times as he spoke again, arrogance oozing from him.

"Don't care. They're just other dudes, I'm not interested."

I pinched my nose. This was going to be a long, long session.

"Mr. Blaznik, what was your intent with calling me here? I assume you have more to say than just hurling insults? I was made to understand you had a sin to confess?"

He shifted and scratched his crotch as he spat on the floor.

"Mmm, maybe I did, maybe I didn't. You know, you'd be a lot hotter if you dropped the pretense that you're intelligent or in any way authoritative. Women are far more desirable when they're just silent and agreeable."

Instead of responding, I decided to simply write down some notes onto my ledger, making the occasional glance up before passing them over to Buck and Nestor to observe.

"Why are you ignoring me?" He leaned forward and let his jaw go slack, hands hanging over his thighs. I continued to pass nonsensical notes with comments like, "smile and chuckle while glancing up at him briefly."

It only took him three minutes to fly into a rage, picking up a piece of furniture from his makeshift room and hurling it at the plexiglass with a thunderous boom.

"You think you're better than me, you fucking skank?! Why? Because you're pretty? Because you're smart? Bitch, I have an IQ of 186, I lift weights for this sculpted body, and I can *have* anyone and *do* anything. I don't need you! Get the fuck out of my sight! NOW!" he bellowed, spit flying from his mouth, face beetroot red.

"Sounds good. We can go out, live our lives, and do great things. Plus, it seems your sin isn't worth eating anyway. The inmates across the way have *far* more delectable sins." I walked to the door and held on to the handle. It was easy to ascertain this poor boy's sin.

His face may have been red from anger, but his sin was green with envy.

And I intend to play him like a fiddle.

"W-wait. My sin *is* worthy. Just... just listen and I'll tell you. I'm sorry, madame... I'm so sorry." He trembled, getting down to his knees and clasping his hands together as if he were a pitiful anime character. "Please forgive my transgressions. You're a queen. I should've controlled myself better!"

It was pathetic, but not surprising for a manipulator. I took my hand off the door and sat back down. Edgar cawed as Holden apologised for waking him up.

"SAD BOY. SAD BOY." He chirped as Holden threw a piece of meat to placate him. I saw Ethan's eyebrow twitch, but he didn't break his stance until I was fully seated.

"Your file says you're a remarkable programmer. A former 'white hat', efficient at taking down any rival who opposed you, and boasting a 4.0 GPA and a scholarship to any university you wanted. You came from privilege and were intent on pursuing a promising career... the hell happened to you?" Buck let the paper fall flat in disbelief as he stroked his beard. Ethan looked him up and down, putting his hand to his patchy bearded face, anger rushing over him until I interjected.

"Ethan, honey, keep your focus on me. Buck is my friend and just like Nestor over there, he's here to help. Can you do that?" I was never an expert at charming people, but I put on my sweetest tone and most sincere smile, which seemed to work. He relaxed and let out a side grin.

"Of course. Mr. Simon McGraw of the fabled McGraw clan of cryptozoologists isn't the least bit threatening anyway, even if his beard is better than mine. I'll get my own eventually, bigger and better than yours. And I bet I know way more about monsters than he does, seen enough of 'em in my time…" He grumbled, fumbling with his hands. "So many fucking animals on the internet that make me look tame by comparison."

"What have you seen, Ethan? What turned you into the person you are today?" I asked gently.

"Let's start with social media. It's a toxic, vacuous black hole from which nothing can escape. You see something, you take a photo and post it. Showing it off to all your adoring fans. Shit they can never even afford or hope to have for themselves. From money to bitche—er, women, and everything in between. It's posturing, and it's sick." He snorted and averted his eyes from mine. "So many friends getting married, having kids, successful jobs… shit I could never dream of. It wasn't fair. It *isn't* fair. But that's not the worst of it."

"Go on, we're listening." I tapped my fingers rhythmically on the table, hoping this wasn't going to turn my stomach.

"Y'see, you can get all sorts of shit on the dark web. Anything, really. I made some good friends there, my brothers in arms. Thought they understood what I was going through. The group I was closest to was The Terrapin System, a group of like-minded young men dedicated to rooting out problematic individuals. Proud 'Thot Patrollers.' We were so good at what we did."

"Sorry, thot patrollers? I'm not sure I understand." I interjected, sure it was a derogatory slur of some kind.

"Say you date a girl and she's had multiple partners. Maybe a dozen or so. Think of it like a shoe, okay? Why would I, a clear alpha, want to buy a shoe that's been used and stretched as opposed to a fresh shoe never worn before? That is what the thot patrol is all about. Finding these disgusting women and shaming them. But we didn't stop there! We'd harass them, stalk them, ensure they never got to feel safe until they publicly apologised and renounced their evil ways." He stopped and a wide grin ran across his face, eyes alight with passion. "It was such a beautiful time. Until the incident…"

He got up and walked toward a whiteboard obscured in the background, tracing his fingers across it before wheeling it over to us.

It was full of photos, some appropriate model shots and others far less pleasant. Side glances of someone as they walked home, unassuming shots of someone sleeping, showering, or eating. My skin crawled and my breath shortened. I knew this kind of horrific behaviour all too well, this level of obsession that would send any sane woman running to a police station if she knew.

Every photo, all the same young woman.

"I met SirenSarah2213 on a stream one night while I was bored. Her stream was barely populated, and she was going on some tangent about female purity, being unfair to men, and being nicer to everyone. Man, she looked sexy as hell in a cosplay outfit. I felt an instant connection and reached out to her, donating to her stream so she'd notice me. Whenever she'd say my name and ask me something, I felt validated." He looked at us, his head tilted to the side with a vacant look in his eyes. "Do you know what it's like for someone to look at you and *see* you, Miss Lockwood? I mean, since your mother, of course."

I felt a sharp stabbing sensation rush through my stomach, but I didn't want to stop his flow, so I simply nodded and motioned for him to continue.

"I ended up spending nearly three thousand dollars on her. By the time the final donation went out, she was doing one-on-one streams with me and giving me "life advice." Saying that my methods with the Terrapins weren't strong enough, that they weren't who they said they were. She pushed me to dig into them and when I finally did, she was right. Most of them had families, friends, partners, and even kids… they had fucking *kids*. How could they understand our methods if they were with loving partners?!"

He bellowed, tears in his eyes.

"I found their secret chat where they mocked me, called me a kissless virgin, and the king of the incels. Hundreds of memes about me with my body photoshopped onto unflattering edits or doge memes directly ripping into my personal views and experiences. It was unbelievably damaging. When I told Siren about it, she soothed me to sleep and promised to show me how to get revenge. That I would be the purest knight this world had ever seen, with her by my side. She even said that we could be together when my job was completed. Can you believe that? I was so lucky, but at the same time, I *knew* it was right. I am an alpha male and nothing would change that."

There was a pause as he looked closely over at Nestor, half cradling Edgar as he ate quietly, his body language still tensed up in case of a fight. Ethan's smile faded, and he walked over to the far side of the glass, sizing Nestor up.

"Hey Holden, you Jewish?" He asked, disgust in his voice. Nestor's eyes flashed, but he kept his cool.

"What if I am?" He asked, his hand still softly petting Edgar. Ethan shook his head.

"Pity. Waste of good muscle." He spat again and walked back over to me.

Nestor continued. "It's all bullshit anyway, Mr. Blaznik. At least in my line of work, everyone ends up in the same place. No matter what god, goddess, or demon you pray to. It ain't worth shit when you're in front of Lady Death."

Ethan exploded at this, the double standards beginning to shine through.

"*My* religion is pure. It's the truest path through God and Jesus. And I heard about your 'line of work,' total fucking fake news; you think I'd buy for a second you work for Lady Death? Fuck off, if Death is a woman, she's the biggest thot going. Stupid cunt."

He was beginning to fly into a rage again and, not wishing to breach both his racist views and the depths of their religious ideologies, I stepped in to keep him focused.

"Ethan, your sin. What did Siren tell you to do next?" I was sensing a pattern in these encounters. Ethan took a breath and sank back into his beanbag.

"She began appearing in my dreams. Which was weird, but she gave me remarkable instructions and tools to take them down one by one. Addresses for their homes, names of their loved ones, methods to enact my revenge."

"And it's at this point you began your 'crusade' against injustice, correct?" Buck asked. Ethan refused to look at him as he nodded in my direction.

"I began with a test run on the newest member. He was easy to locate since he never deviated from his pattern. He'd never seen me in person, so when I posed as a Mormon looking to give him some info on the book of Joseph Smith, he never batted an eyelid. The guy even invited me into his home, big mistake. The second his door locked, I smashed his brains in with a claw hammer. It was then that Siren spoke to me again."

He looked wistfully up at the ceiling, pausing before continuing. Was he ashamed? Or was he revelling in the moment?

"She said: 'They took everything from you. Now take something you wanted from them.' So, I looked at this fallen piece of meat, Darrel, I think his name was. I looked at him and asked myself what I wanted most. Well, Darrel had a beautiful home despite his new status to the group, so I took that. Easy enough to move in and assume his bills. The guy was a shut-in and nobody questioned it when I took over."

A thick green mist was now covering the surrounding floor. It looked noxious, but Ethan paid it no mind.

"How did she talk to you?" I asked, his attention lapsing and almost looking offended that I'd stopped him mid flow.

"What? Why does that matter? She was there when I needed her, as she always was." He retorted, bile in his words.

"It matters to me, I can't eat your sin if I don't know everything. You wouldn't want to lie to me, would you? I'm not as clever as I look." I felt disgust at my own deprecation, but this was part of the job, so I stuck with it. His expression softened, and he carried on.

"Fine, fine. I can't excuse a lady being honest. Siren wasn't a normal girl, she was radiant, alluring, and always there when I needed her. I mean that literally. After I'd donated to her enough, the one-on-one sessions began, and she manifested in front of me. I could never touch her, but I could always see her as clear as I see you. She was instrumental in my growth and as we proceeded, she only got clearer to me. After a couple more targets, I'd taken their car and bank accounts, but the last one was where things got complicated."

He paused again, and I exchanged a look with Buck; I didn't like where this was going. The haze was beginning to form the shape of a woman, a bowl.

"See, Siren told me not to listen to anything they said, to keep my mind focused on what they had that I didn't. That this would be one of the final steps to ascension. She gave me something to drink and for a moment, our fingers brushed... I felt electricity run through us. So, I did as I was told, drank from the bowl and ignored everything until I reached the master bedroom. I felt… different. My vision tunnelled and a green haze fell over my eyes as my fists acted on their own. My clawhammer was tossed aside as I strangled the person in front of me, seeing visions of the life they led that I was denied. The laughter of all my colleagues in the group, happy couples, and the entire fucking world judging me. All of them just filling up my skull until it threatened to burst like the stupid cunts in front of me as my grip grew tighter… and tighter… until…"

He stopped, motioning the bursting of a balloon and contents spilling out.

"No more. I felt as if I'd constricted them into submission. Become the true alpha now that the leader of the pack. But no, instead I was looking down at a total stranger—a woman, in fact."

"You were looking down at the woman you'd been thirsting for all this time, weren't you, Blaznik?" Buck sighed, venom in his words. "Saoirse Maisey Lovejoy, nineteen-year-old streamer and model. You'd been paying to get her attention and one night you flew into a rampage when she banned you from the server, got her info and that of your contemporaries when they tried to stop you."

He held up a photo as the mist began forming, the two matching up perfectly. A beautiful woman with flowing red hair, the photo showing a cosplay of Poison Ivy from the Batman comics. The woman now formed in the room, clad in an emerald green dress that hung at the shoulder, clutching a large bowl with a bubbling liquid.

"No… that's not… I didn't…"

"Saoirse, Indiviosa…" Buck said, getting up to slam the photo against the wall and make him look as her counterpart walked toward him. "Saoirse, abounding in envy. You never had a siren calling to you, Blaznik, never had a larger-than-life plan fit for an alpha mastermind. Your jealousy simply overwhelmed you, created a narrative where you were in control and had it all. Well, you're going to live out your sin whether you want to or not. You will spend your final moments knowing you can never have what you want."

I looked at my own plate and saw two dishes form. One was a side of Mexican bean rice with green peppers, the other was a Glamorgan sausage and Yorkshire pudding—the way my mum made it. The *exact* way she made it. It even smelled the same. I felt an overwhelming rush of emotions and nostalgic memories, desperately fighting toward the surface with the first bite.

But I couldn't reach for it. Even if I wanted to.

Eyes fixated on the unfolding carnage in front of me, my body acted on its own and began shovelling the rice into my mouth as the sausage and Yorkshire faded from view, lovingly being consumed by something unseen. I watched with anger and misery as the meal I wanted was once again fading from my grasp.

After a few moments of staring, Ethan turned to see the visage of his siren in front of him. Her expression was that of pure satisfaction as she used her free hand to point down at the floor in a domineering fashion. He whimpered and obliged, head pressed against the ground as he shook.

"I only wanted what was mine. Isn't that fair? Isn't that a man's duty to claim what is rightfully his? I don't understand... is this ascension? Or punishment? I don't... I don't..."

He raised his head to look at the visage of Saoirse as she tipped the contents of the bowl over him and into his mouth, partially widened in a scream that would never be uttered.

The green liquid ate at his skin with remarkable speed, flesh bubbling and popping as it splattered across the plexiglass, his rapidly decaying torso shuddering and eyes melting into the sockets as he gurgled until slumping over.

I was less focused on his pain and more so on my own. This sin did not physically encumber me, make me sick, or wear me out. No, instead it bore into my soul and found a small place to nest next to the memories of my mother that I kept with me every day.

It managed to shake my professionalism and my confidence, something nobody had done before.

With more of these fucking monsters to go, I was unsure I was up for the task and began to doubt my abilities.

As if on cue, the same spectral night terror that has plagued me since my arrival shone in the viscera of the plexiglass, standing right behind me with a malformed digit up to its cracked lips in a hush motion. In its other hand it held the totem I'd been given by Nestor as a safekeeping method from god knows what. I watched as this thing crushed it to dust, holding up a number as a shock wave ran through my body, fear buckling my knees.

Something in the prison stirred at my presence, something I would come to fear more than any other creature in existence.

"Four."

Inmate #2122: *Ethan Elliot Blaznik III*
Sin: *Envy*
Food: *Mexican bean rice. The one dish I will always want, but will never have again.*

The Fourth Sin: Acedia (Sloth)

I'm about to meet my next inmate, a person steeped in negligence, self-righteousness, and laziness. I ruminated on how this visit had already led me to a lustrous woman who liquified her victims into a "cure all" tonic for love—including her own daughter, a pair of twins so besotted by greed that they were willing to stitch their family together to get what they wanted, and a man filled with such envious rage that he brutally took the lives of people who had things he wished he did.

Now, I'm preparing to stare down a woman who is synonymous with the kind of negligence and abhorrence of kindness that'd make anyone's stomach turn.

But before we get to that, we have to address the elephant in the room: the warden. I'm aware some of his behaviour indicates that he isn't to be trusted. From his namesake, to the way Edgar behaved around him, and the seeming happiness to pull the plug on the whole operation when I didn't wake up.

I aimed to confront him, requesting permission to go to his office from one of the guards after a short nap and time to decompress. I didn't talk to Buck, Nestor, or anyone about how the grief of losing my mother bubbled to the surface after finishing the last meal. There was no point when it was written all over my face, tears streaming down my face as we finished up and left the room. Buck simply hugged me as I sobbed before leaving me time to heal as he went off to "explore the prison and gain intel" while Nestor went topside to give Edgar some room to fly, not wanting him to be cooped up too long.

After riding the lengthy elevator for a solid fifteen minutes, I came to a long marble hallway with huge portraits of Greek gods doing battle. There was Saturn eating his own son, the imprisonment of titans in Tartarus, and the violent affairs that occurred on Earth before Zeus flooded the planes. Every portrait was more macabre in nature as I ventured closer to the large chamber doors that housed the warden's office.

No receptionist to greet me, I simply knocked and waited for a response. Hearing frantic murmuring from behind the door and a soft song playing, I knocked again and cracked the door ajar to try

The Last Sin Eater

and call a little louder but within acceptable volume, not wanting to cause offence if he was in a meeting.

And when I looked in, I could tell he most certainly was in a meeting.

Just not the kind I'd have expected.

In the centre of a grand room was a prisoner, chained inside a large barrel. They were submerged up to the waist in the murky waters of a pool that stretched to fifty feet in diameter. Small critters of all shapes and sizes sloshed about underneath the obscured surface. Two high-ranking officials stood on either side of the barrel, taking notes and observing the warden, now without his trench coat on. Instead, he sported a silver waistcoat, black and gold sigils across it with a white shirt underneath, sleeves rolled up to reveal lengthy verses written in what I assumed was Germanic. His tall frame was leaner than I anticipated, not an ounce of fat on his arms or his torso. The man clearly took care of himself.

"Now, inmate #855, you have been with mein establishment for quite some time, yes? I have done mein best to keep you comfortable, respect du, and ensure no harm befell you. I have done mein job as einen warden to keep you safe and you repay me mit... this?"

He brandished a shank in front of the man, crafted from toothbrushes and a carving knife, dipped in poison and sharp to the touch. The man thrashed in his barrel, but didn't respond.

"You know, I take great pride in this prison, for we only house der worst of der worst. Die prisoners that nobody else wants. Ein outcasts!" He threw the shank at the wall. It stuck out, shaking as a grin flashed across his face. He leaned in close and cocked his head to the side as he lightly slapped the prisoner's face. "Du. Are. Nicht. Wanted. Und Du. Are. Nicht. Loved."

He turned his back, arms crossed behind him and staring out of his bay window. A grand view over the general population of his expansive prison, so many types of individuals roaming the floors that were clearly not human: lycanthropes, ursine warriors, wendigos, haired apes, and regular humans all cavorted as if it were normal. He sighed and continued talking as his two associates began walking around, pouring something into the slots, I could smell the sickly scent of milk and honey, mellified man rising to the surface and making me want to retch. But, I resisted, my horror rooting me to the spot.

They were slathering him up as bait.

"Does du know about Scaphism, 855? It is one of das worst ways to be taken out of this world. You are offered up into dirty water rife with parasites, insects, carnivorous fish and mammals that are attracted to your soft, delicious flesh. They will eat you bit by bit, piece by piece, and you will rot for days before death comes to claim your sorry soul."

The inmate finally broke their silence to protest.

"I was trying to defend myself! Those blacks, you know what they're like on the outside—you must understand my safety! The safety of our race!"

But the warden held up his hand and shook his head.

"Let us get something correct, Herr Roofedge. I may be German, but I took this job to capture and eliminate people like you. I have no interest in your ideas of racial purity and your appeal to my skin colour insults us both. Overstepping my absolute ruling is a slight ich cannot ignore, I have more self respect than that. Besides…" He turned and looked at me, smiling.

"You offended our sin eater. If you weren't a dead man before, you are now."

He clicked his fingers and the two assistants submerged the barrel in the water, leaving only his head exposed and covered by a bag to muffle the inmate's pleas for clemency. The structure was then wheeled out of the room and past me. The warden smiled warmly as I shuffled awkwardly inside his study.

"I hope this shows that despite mein cold exterior, I do have a moral compass, Frau Lockwood." He gestured to the window, and I walked over to join him. "We house all manner of social offenders here, from those who harm people on racial and gender prejudices to child harmers and so forth. Nobody escapes our grasp and nobody ever will. But, I feel I have lost your trust and so must be candid…"

He pointed to a cell at the bottom of the general population where a large hole resided, every single inmate avoiding it like the plague as they congregated. I picked up the scent of wildflowers, the taste of elderberries, and a sensation of pure unadulterated hatred emanating from that point.

Something lurked in there. Something old and powerful. Eyes unseen pierced through the darkness and tore into me, shaking my resolve to its core.

"You sense it too, ja? That will be Prisoner 001, our first inmate. Some would say der leader of this prison, if you exclude me, of course. They've been here since the earliest days and you will meet them when the time is right."

"They're not on death row?" I asked, swallowing the lump in my throat. His aura was overwhelming and I had to turn away.

"Not exactly. But that's not the question you came here to ask, is it, Frau Lockwood?" He walked over to his drink cabinet and picked out a bottle—black and in a casket, chains wrapped around the structure in a ceremonial manner, the front reading "The Hunter's Dream; for when your rest is nowhere in sight." He poured two whiskey glasses full of the red and black liquid, dropping a white circular block of ice within, almost like pure moonlight amid the cloak of night in the drink.

"Why do we need to eat the sins of these fucking monsters?" I asked, a bead of sweat rushing down my temple as I turned away and reached for the glass. The warden sat in his recliner, sloshing the drink around wistfully before he answered.

"And so comes the time where I must be candid, Frau Lockwood—there is a greater reason for your work here. One that will determine so many things beyond you, me, this prison and the outside world. When I say you are doing the work of the gods, I mean it."

I downed the drink in one, the burning sensation lining my throat and waking me from a fear-addled malaise immediately. Before I could ask, he held up a hand.

"Ah, not for now. I must ask you to trust me on this, but you will learn in due time. However, I know trust must be regained and so I offer you this."

He pulled a document from his desk and slid it over. A headshot of a young woman with flowing black hair obscuring half her face, a scowl written across the remainder as pierced lips and gritted teeth glare up at me.

"Prisoner #6626, Luciana Maria DeSantos. Twenty-one-year-old head of the Church of the Duskwalkers, responsible for the Sturgeon Day of Reckoning."

He slid a newspaper in front of me, the headline reading:

"MASSACRE AT STURGEON UTALITARIAN CHURCH; HUNDREDS DEAD IN MASS SUICIDE."

A photo accompanying it showcased a sea of bodies hidden over tarps, sneakers and shoes sticking out from the bottom as a crowd gathered outside, frozen in screams of bloody murder.

So many of the shoes were child sizes.

Among them would be an old friend from when I moved to Sturgeon, someone I lost contact with so long ago.

The first friend I made in the city.

"I understand you know of this individual? Someone du ist familiar with back home?" He asked. My expression clearly betraying my desire to show stoicism, I nodded. "Well, then, I wish for you to know something. You will get very little out of her. She is the most uncooperative of our death row inmates. Only when you show her this will you get the response you need and a relatively painless experience."

He slid me a note, sealed with the prison sigil and a warning attached to the front, stipulating not to open unless necessary.

"I hope this can mend bridges and assuage concern, Frau Lockwood. I carry great pride in this prison. I wish for its reputation to stay intact—whatever the case."

-

Heading back downstairs, I was escorted by the guards straight to the visitation area, despite not being with Buck or Nestor. I protested, but the guards simply shook their heads, saying it was time for the interview.

I patted myself down and felt a small lump in the inside pocket of my jacket. The totem perhaps? Maybe that creature didn't get it after all. Either way, I had little time to deliberate as I was taken to the main interview room. It was bathed in blue light and there was soft piano playing. The scent of gouda cheese and wine wafted through the cracks of the door.

I stepped in, feeling remarkably vulnerable for the first time without my trusted friends and guides, but confident in my knowledge that of all the people we'd faced thus far, this one was someone I could handle.

After all, I at least knew her.

And what she did.

Luciana came into Sturgeon a penniless, destitute, and drug-addled woman from the slums. No mother to speak of, and the less said of her father, the better. When she was fourteen, she ran away from home and began giving street corner sermons. She was determined to help others see what she saw in the world: a flood of people lost in the shuffle, going about their days without cause for concern or a direction. So many were lying to themselves about their beliefs, saying one thing and doing another, praying their way into Heaven while rapidly crawling into the tight crevasse that was the gateway to Purgatory with their deeds.

She offered them a question: What if you were just *honest* with yourself? If you lived life the way you were supposed to, saw the things you eschewed, what wonders would open up to you?

Luciana spoke of visions from her youth, as so many prophets do, declaring Belphegor sat on his throne of municipal waste. While so many describe him as being on the toilet, Luciana said he sat on the gateway to a better life, only letting those who truly embodied his ideals and that of the greater gods through to meet them. He was a gatekeeper.

In her first town, she was cast out. Many viewed her as blasphemous, heretical, and saw no place for a woman to speak her mind on religious ideals. Her story truly came alive once she stepped foot into Sturgeon some two years later at just sixteen years old. She said a man who stood where air could do naught but fester, and smells dulled to a point of absence, offered her a check, an establishment, and a new title: Mother Accumulator.

So, the church flourished in a building steeped in dusk at all times. St. Martin's Utilitarian Church. Every member that joined would go indoors, be given a thick robe, and then taken blindfolded through a cavern to a small area steeped in twilight. Revellers and fanatics said the sun was hidden behind a black moon, the entire congregation bathed in a twilight glow that invigorated them, emboldened them to do things they'd never do, to reject their old traditions and gods.

Still, to think this woman was responsible for The Day Of Reckoning... it was shocking.

Looking at her now, lying in a softly swaying hammock and wrapped up in a fluffy blanket, softly drinking wine and looking like a normal millennial, her appearance was almost a total dichotomy from the person printed in the papers. I took my seat and rolled up my sleeves, tied my locks back into a bun, and ensured I was prepared. I had a feeling this would test me.

"Ms. DeSantos, my name is Miss Lockwood. You called upon my services in order to eat your sins before your end. I must apologise that my colleagues are not with me, they appear to be engaged elsewhere. But I feel we know one another well enough to proceed without them. Is that okay?"

Silence. She glanced over once before swirling her wine and downing it in one go; the glass filling up again as she set it down. Unseen hands catered to her every whim. I sighed.

"You also go by the name Mother Accumulator, do you not? Head of The Church of the Duskwalkers, an organisation I am, unfortunately, most familiar with." I paused, thinking of that first friend. She was almost like an aunt to me, her door always open when I needed advice, the coffee shop she owned forever bustling with happy guests, would be artists, and philosophers debating until closing time. Abigail Priestley was a gifted orator, expert coffee brewer, and lover of all animals, her bearded dragon Montgomery always on her shoulder and crawling under her thick blonde hair whenever he got scared.

In time, she would struggle with financial woes as Sturgeon faced an economic downturn. She took to wandering the streets at night, hoping for answers to her problems. When a local outreach member of the church hailed her down, that was that. She became Duskwalker Abbie, and within six months, she would be...

No, I had to focus.

"Ms. DeSantos, this procedure cannot work without your cooperation. The other inmates di—"

She waved a hand at me, twirling finely manicured fingers in a far less subdued manner than Mr. Blaznik's condescending finger wag. She merely didn't want me to continue for the sake of it.

"I'm not them. They're not me. We're all different in this place and while I did call you, I had a change of heart. The gods say you're not the one, and I follow their behest. If you cannot prove your importance, then I'll simply have to fail at my task and die here, unfulfilled."

My eyebrows raised at that. Failed at her task? A small stream of blue smoke began to pile in from the top of her enclosure—not enough to manifest anything, but it was a start.

"Your followers all died at your behest. Wasn't that your great task, getting them all to ascension?"

She scoffed, then took a delicate bite of some tiramisu and wiped her lips with a napkin. She breathed softly and let her slender frame sink further into the hammock, not bothering to lift her head to look up at me.

"That's what the media assumed. Maybe that's what some of the newbies believed, those just looking for a cause to die for. But no, every initiated follower knew exactly what we were doing. We were preparing *me*. Preparing *my* body for the next stage. I simply had to lift a hand, and they did as I asked. The laziest mass murderer this world has ever seen. My numbers do not simply exist within the halls of St. Martin's. No, we had cells all over, and they will continue to wake up and do what is written until the number is sufficiently high enough. I have nothing to do now but wait for the next step. Wait for my rightful throne in the stars."

The mist began to pool around the back corner, forming a large seat, something shaking on top of it, and small, thin hands clutching at the bottom as if trying to reach up to the seat.

"You say you're different from the others, but I sense similarities in you all. Each of you having a guide, a purpose, a chance to ascend. There's more going on here than simply letting you die, isn't there?" I sat up, preparing to walk to the door. "I will not be a pawn in someone else's game, even if the warden says otherwise. You can rot here for all I care."

As I took steps to the door, her lackadaisical voice cooed after me.

"Do you know where you go when you die? I do. I know where everyone goes."

Something made my hand freeze on the door handle, luminous eyes rushed into my mind as if something else was watching me. I felt compelled to turn around and continue, sitting back down with a sigh.

"I'm listening, go on." I replied, the smell of gouda beginning to overwhelm my nostrils and eradicate my love of cheese. She smiled and raised her head for the first time.

"That's not how it works. Make an offering to me, to the church. If it's good enough, I'll consider it." She took another bite and swallowed a large helping of wine. I sighed.

I was either going to be her soundboard or get this done, unsure of what I could even ask to progress beyond her sermons.

Then I remembered the note the warden had given me.

Giving pause for just a moment, I grabbed it, and heeded the words on top. "Let her read it first." I unsealed it and, as the instructions stipulated, held it up to the plexiglass for her to read.

Immediately, her demeanour changed. She dropped the cheese and wine and hopped out of her hammock, rushing over to read it carefully, tracing each line with her finger and gazing at what appeared to be a picture at the bottom. Tears filled her eyes and the corners of her mouth curled into a wide smile of uproarious joy as she leaned back, wiping her eyes.

"Your offering is most acceptable, Madame Lockwood. I will tell you everything and impart some advice to you before the end." She walked over to the wall opposite her hammock and began painting. Materials appeared out of nowhere, as deft hands swiped across a plain canvas, her elegance never faltering when she spoke.

"When did your lord appear to you?" I asked, trying to cast my mind back to what Buck had taught me about tulpas and their embodiments of our sins.

"I was just a little girl when he appeared in front of me on a throne made of bone, sinew, and the figures of so many trying to hold his frame up comfortably. Countless little bodies, hands and legs straining to make him happy, his body hovering over the portal to the better place. They wanted so badly to be let in, to gain favour, but he offered that only to me. He said I carried greatness within me and must go out, follow his instructions, and stay on the path. Being charismatic and beautiful certainly helped, as well as the offerings of one of my lords, who provided sanctuary and financial security. Our following grew exponentially after that, especially when we could talk the talk and walk the walk."

She paused, grabbing a deep shade of red paint, and chuckling.

"When we first showed the new initiates the stars and what devoured them, their joy was rare and magnificent. It was an understanding of their placement in this world and the realisation that all they had to do in order to see the next step was serve me."

The blue mist had crawled up the entire back wall, scaling to nearly twelve feet in height. More bodies piled at the base of this metallic seat, their faces permanently frozen in agony under the crushing weight.

"So you put things in place for Sturgeon's Day of Reckoning. A cool summer day in August when the sun set and the moon had not yet risen. The city would wake up to a sight that would be felt across the world. We all know this and this isn't your sin to confess, so let's get right to it—what is it they didn't know? What happened to the congregation? To my friend Abbie?" I regretted saying it the moment her name left my lips, but I couldn't help myself. Luciana's face fell for a moment and she picked up a yellow, bright and warm like Abbie's hair.

"Ah, Duskwalker Abbie, one of our trusted priestesses. She was so dedicated to the group after her life took a turn. I'm… sorry that she couldn't say goodbye before the end. You were an outsider. You were not to know. If I have one regret, it's that I inadvertently slighted someone of your stature and lineage. We prepared a concoction in line with Lord Belphegor's teachings, a poison that would steadily dim the light inside in time with the last etches of light on the horizon. They would go to sleep and within minutes be gone."

A large horned figure took shape on the throne, a hand resting under its chin while the other pushed on its legs, a scowl across its face not dissimilar to that of Luciana's mugshot. She began to paint faster, with more purpose and less elegance.

"The poison was willingly ingested by every member of our group. Over seven hundred souls willing to go with the sun and leave before the moon realised they'd departed. Deep underground where the twilight shone, we basked in the light and I watched from my throne as they all praised me, praised Belphegor, praised our all-mother and the unnameable ones. They fell into a deep sleep and I was left to watch and wait, knowing this would be my final home. But…"

"Wait, aren't *you* Mother Accumulator?" I asked, not wishing to interject but unable to ignore such an admission. She threw a stroke with her brush across the obscured canvas, the colours practically glowing from it and bathing her in a strange hue.

"I am. But she is Omnium Matrem. The woman who founded our movement and was there on the first day of operations at the behest of our lord. She was no longer with us by the time that I took over, but her spirit was always an influence. Of course, there were complications—the poison did not react the same in everyone. I would guess a third of the congregation did slumber. Another third were quiet, but visibly unable to find any respite, and the last group screamed, writhing and gurgling as the poison wreaked havoc on their bodies. Belphegor told me this was my own test. He instructed me to do something that would cement my legacy as the church's finest ruler."

The mist had finished forming. A red-horned ogre sat atop a bone throne with countless damned souls either trying to hold him up, escape, or get into the black hole his body hovered over. It was easy to see how it was misinterpreted as a toilet, but all I saw was a throne literally built on the labours of those who had worked for him.

At the same time, my plate started to fill up, and my stomach growled. The sins we eat do not ever add onto our actual diet and we never retain the food, but for the time we smell, taste, touch, and eat it, it's real. My stomach could not have been happier as eyes met the growing plate.

The most succulent feast: bacon-wrapped filet mignon with a French cabernet, a wheel of various brie, gouda, and blue cheese, potatoes au gratin, with a molten chocolate cake for dessert. I knew there had to be something unpleasant to it, but my hunger did not care. The job was not quite done, however, and I was determined to see this one through.

"What did you do, Luciana? What did you do that truly put you in this place and with this sin of sloth?"

She finished her painting, tying her matted black hair back and placing her hands on her hips. She turned it toward me, temporarily blinding me with its brilliance and the sheer light from the luminescent paint.

"I walked amid the sea of the dead. I saw so many at peace, but so many more still struggling to reach that goal. Children and babies were screaming out for their mothers, for me… but I simply looked down at them with pity and did nothing but observe as they struggled. All children of the dusk must walk that path on their own. I watched many pass over that threshold, and did not leave until I knew each member of my flock had transcended. That is true godhood. That is the legacy of Luciana Maria DeSantos, Mother Accumulator of The Church of the Duskwalkers, bringer of The Day of Reckoning and, most importantly…"

My eyes adjusted to the painting as an alarm began ringing out, sirens blaring throughout the facility. The warden's panicked voice called over the tannoy.

"ACHTUNG! ATTENTION! INMATE #5933 HAS CAPTURED TWO OF OUR GUESTS. THIS FACILITY IST IN LOCKDOWN. FRAU LOCKWOOD, PLEASE REPORT TO CENTRAL WING IMMEDIATELY; THEY WILL NOT SPEAK WITH US!"

Buck, Nestor… that's why they hadn't turned up.

I wish I could have reacted in that moment, gotten up to rush to their aid. My eyes were adjusting to the painting in front of me and the image of Luciana walking, without any reservations, to the back of the room where Belphegor sat, still towering over her petite frame even when sat down.

"It was the utmost pleasure that I got to find out who you truly were, where you came from, Madame Lockwood. Your mother did great things for us, truly great things. A word of advice: if you let it in, it will take everything. Good luck, we'll see one another again. Maybe in a bar between spaces."

I could not take my eyes off of the painting. My hands shovelled the food into my mouth mechanically without pause for thought or concern. The sounds of Luciana being pulled apart and shoved into the hole in the seat filled my ears with naught a scream or groan from her. She accepted her fate as an observer, sick as she may be.

The painting was that of my mother. Young and beautiful as I remembered her, her afro large, and with a pink comb embedded in the side that I constantly used to play with. She was laughing, dressed in a pair of dungarees, and holding a younger me on her shoulder. Around her neck was a large pendant with a keyhole over a locket, a sigil synonymous with The Church of the Duskwalkers and a title engraved in the top:

"To Omnium Matrem; E Dolore Magna Gloria…"

I knew that phrase. It was the same one both my mother and grandmother repeatedly drilled into me when things got tough. A phrase the Lockwood family kept close and was not known outside of that context. How did she know?

The food began to rot in my mouth. Looking down at the leftovers of the food, I saw creatures crawling through the remnants. Festering, pulsing decay infused with the popping maggots and fungus. The fetid stench reminded me it was the result of one's laziness and the efforts of others.

Tears in my eyes from the horrific food, the overwhelming fear of my friends' safety pushing me to rush, and the horrific realisation my mother—my idol—was not what she seemed. I spoke the Latin phrase aloud in English and tearfully swallowed the last bite before rushing to save my friends.

-

Inmate #6626: *Luciana Maria DeSantos aka "Mother Accumulator" for The Church of the Duskwalkers.*
Sin: *Sloth*
Food: *A gourmet of delights rotted due to negligence and inaction, built off the back of the others.*

"Through great pain comes glory."

The Fifth Sin: Gula (Gluttony)

As soon as I finished dealing with the subtle evil that was sloth, I was on my way to dealing with a far more pressing issue: someone taking my friends hostage and holding them for ransom.

The wait in the elevator was excruciating. It had always been long, but had it always been *this* long? I couldn't tell, but with every passing floor and stream of light rushing through the tube window, my anxiety built upon itself. The elevator may as well have been filled with water up to my neck for how much I paced, thrashed, and ruminated on the worst.

After an age, the doors clattered open, and I stormed toward central, a stoic warden waiting for me with his sleeves up and hands in his pockets.

"Ah! Frau Lockwood, danke for getting here so quickly, I was most concerned you'd be held up by th—"

I breezed past him to the view in front of me, a large plexiglass screen that displayed the carnage down below in an extra large enclosure: bodies on pikes, split open and hollowed out, teeth smashed inward to the gums, noses removed from faces and barely any living soul amid the sea of inmates ripped to pieces.

That is, of course, aside from the man situated at the end of a great circular table. He was gigantic, but not in the way Tallulah, the woman who represented lust was. His weight was, for the most part, distributed better. Thighs like tree trunks, arms great hulking amorphous bulges of muscle, his barrel chest stretching out to double my own width, and a great beard flowing down to his navel. His stomach shivered and rumbled incessantly as he took mounds of food from his plate and shovelled them into a huge mouth, emitting horrific sounds as he dined, paired with vile lip smacking and tongue licking against the vestiges of food in his mouth without concern for decorum. Despite the window, I could hear every bite, every chew and swallow.

But it was when I saw his plate that the fear set in, knowing full well this one was going to be different from the others.

It was stained in dark blood, a piece of leg still uneaten but barely anything left amid the surrounding bones. He peered down with frustration, pushing his chair back to walk over to a poor soul on a makeshift pike in the corner, thankfully not impaled yet, but instead chained to it by the top, partially obscured by the poor lighting.

"You've got sixty seconds to get down here, or I take a piece of him for my protein workout." The low, northern English voice called out, his massive fist reaching for the person's leg. As they resisted, I saw Nestor's defiant eyes look up at me and shake his head.

"Don't, he just wants you for—AGH!"

Blood streamed from his stomach as sharp claws dug in and took a pound of flesh, the larger man holding it above his widening jaws and swallowing in one go. A small trickle of blood rushed down his chin.

"Time's already started, love, hurry up."

I turned on my heel and made a beeline for the stairs as the warden walked with me, shoving a document into my hands.

"Inmate #5933 is Cyril Monks, former underground fighting champion and dealer of a killer drug 'Thanatos.' He's a master manipulator and takes what he wants. I do not advise you go in there without our usual protection, Frau Lockwood. The risks it poses you and the prison are substantial." He pleaded, barely keeping pace with me as we reached the final hallway connecting us to Monks' cell.

"Fuck the risks. Fuck the prison. He wants a face-to-face interview? He'll get one. He should know not to underestimate any of us. I'll look to you to take a shot if anything goes wrong, Warden." I looked at him, a grimace on my face. "I didn't get this far by being a pretty face, I can gut a motherfucker if I need to." He swallowed and nodded.

When I turned back, for the briefest of moments, I saw something from the leftmost guard. His hat drew down low and a salute was offered as we walked past, toward the door.

At least, I thought it was a salute. His fingers were drawn at the brim of his hat, but something was off… there weren't the usual four with the thumb tucked in.

He lifted his head and for a split second, the hand drew down. In front of me, a familiar maniacal grin plastered on his visage burned its way into my skull, the number on his hand doing the same as I passed through to the enclosure:

    Three.

The first scent I picked up was iron. With so much blood and viscera around me, it was impossible not to.

    "They had me waiting with some lower-risk inmates. Thought because I was on good behaviour that I'd do my bit to get better privileges. Even gave me visitation for nine years of no incidents. Imagine their shock when I started pulling limbs from bodies. Cunts never stood a chance, bless 'em." He rested back on the chair, his makeshift lunch table splattered with blood. "C'mon, take a seat, we've got much to discuss."

    I looked at the back end of the room and saw Buck and Nestor on either side, both bloodied and beaten, but not dead or mortally wounded. Breathing a small sigh of relief, I sat down on the opposite end and put my papers down, prepping to introduce myself.

    "You know who I am, I know who you are, so let's not pussyfoot around, eh? I have a way of doing things and you are no exception, Miss Lockwood. If we do this, it's on my terms." He breezed through my introduction as if it was nothing, pulling a dumbbell from the floor and flexing as he spoke. "I will ask you a series of questions and if you answer the way I want you to, you can ask one back. Answer wrong and…" he threw his hand back, thumb pointed toward my two boys. "I'll take a piece of 'em. Literally."

    My hands shook, and I felt a lump in my throat. He wasn't joking. Reluctantly, I smiled and nodded, not enjoying the lack of control I had over this situation.

    "Good. So, what can ya tell me about your upbringing, Nellie?" He leaned back in his chair, imposing frame bearing down on the rickety joints, hands folded over his stomach.

    "First eleven years of my life were good; things were simple at home but pleasant. Mum worked hard and was always busy, but never stopped making time for me no matter what it was. Baking, nature walks, finding and identifying the animals in the woods nearby or whatever else, Mum never stopped trying. Then, I turned twelve and things began to change." I pursed my lips, those painful memories rising to the surface. Arguments, slammed doors, misunderstandings. Typical teenage things that are supposed to be fractals in your life and not the final definitive moments of your last days with your mother. "Well, things were never the same after that. Then, one day, she told me to stay at home while she took a work call. Never came back, and I was looked after by my grandparents. Here we are." I shrugged and shook my head, hating that I was telling all of this to an animal in this prison.

"Good, good. You seem to get it. Ask away." He chuckled, finishing his rep and going on to work the other arm.

"What drove you to be this way? How does a legitimate bodybuilder and family man, according to your file, begin distributing a powerful new drug and tearing people limb from limb?" I furtively scanned over the notes, determined not to take my eyes off of him for too long. He smiled, bright white teeth stained with red.

"Adephagia. Or Adi, if you know her. I tore my ACL and MCL; docs said it'd take eighteen months to get back to any kind of work. That meant watching my colleagues progress beyond me, get bigger and stronger, achieve all the shit that was *mine* to achieve. Less money, less power, less interest." He shook his head, getting up and grabbing a pair of human spines on the floor with some rope attached, using it as a macabre skipping rope as he carried on talking. "I got sick of it. My anger and desire grew into something more and I overheard some boys talking about this new kind of steroid: Thanatos. Fuckers said it was a reawakening in the system, but you had to know the right people to get it. I may have been on crutches, but I still beat the silly cunts until they gave up the info. Met the guy in a supermarket car park at four am, paid him what I had left of my savings, and he dashed off. I barely saw his face in all the excitement. That's where things changed." He finished skipping, the scraping of the vertebrae on the floor making me nauseous.

A thick, pungent golden mist began forming around his body, but he paid it no mind if he knew it was there.

"Your turn. Can you smell and taste your own sins? Do you know what lurks deep within your soul?" He chuckled, grabbing a handful of meat from under the table, opening his mouth before closing it and looking at me quizzically. "Oh, you don't mind if I dine while we whine? Haha." He chuckled, shoving the food in his mouth with those abhorrent sounds even louder as I spoke.

"A lot of people have asked that, but the truth is I sense nothing. Whenever I go into meditation and focus on myself, I can smell, taste, feel nothing of my own sins—though I know they're there."

He shoved his chair firmly away from the table, scowling as he walked over to Buck, grabbing his arm at the wrist. Buck was barely conscious as his head rocked around from the jerking motion.

"I warned you about lying, Nellie." he hissed, roaring as he bit down hard on Buck's entire hand, severing it at the bone as a blood-curdling scream rang out. Cyril savoured the bites and sang in the same pitch as Buck's pain-riddled yells.

I drew my knife, hot blood running through my veins.

"I will fucking end you, right here and now."

But he sat down, acting as if all he'd done was kick over a chair, shaking his head and savouring the last bites of Buck's hand and fingers, crushed between diamond strength molars.

"Nope, you won't. I'm not interested in anything that isn't my own, but I value my life above any of your sad little existences. You so much as get within five feet and I will bite more desirable parts of Buck off, then start at Nestor's legs. Not only are you going to tell the truth on your last statement, but you're going to answer another question as penance. So, try again."

I slammed the table, yelling and trying to catch my breath, failing in the process.

"I... Yes, yes, okay, I once saw my sin. It was cloaked in black, smelled of my mother's cooking and tasted of... nothing. It had a total absence. But I could see it. And it... "

"It looked like the thing that plagues your nightmares? Yes, I know. Thank you. Do you love Buck?" He asked, licking his lips and walking over to a pair of intact corpses hanging from the rafters, punching them as if they were sides of beef to practice boxing on. Swift, precise punches rained down on the poor souls.

Anger gave way to embarrassment and a slew of complex emotions. My initial response was to ask how that was his business, to deflect or give a half answer. But that wouldn't do. This was not a time for complacency or half measures.

"With everything I hold dear. But not just a romantic love. A love that transcends the physical. He was my mentor as a young woman, he treated me like an equal and looks to me for advice now.

He's everything to me. Which makes what you did a moment ago that much more egregious in my eyes." I paused, taking a breath and resigning to deal with the aftermath of my revelation later, thankful in part that Buck had passed out from shock so I was spared the embarrassment. "Now, tell me what brought you here, in full."

Left hook, right hook, uppercut, knee to the groin. Cyril Monk was incessant in his onslaught, as if he had something to prove.

"I tried Thanatos that night. First dosage straight to the veins and it sent a surge through my body that I swear gave me a bloody heart attack. When my senses returned, I was clearly out of it. I stood in this great marble hall that had statues of the greatest warriors and baddest motherfuckers living or dead. At the end, Adi stood. Huge woman, muscled and big in all the right places, stronger than I could ever hope to be. Big jaws on her stomach and a tail the size of my entire body with a hungry mouth at the end. She told me if I could defeat seven other men, take something from them, and defeat her, she'd help me ascend to that true state of power—of dominance. Not a single thing out of my grasp." He volleyed off one last right hook, the ribs of the body caving in and blood spraying over his face. He lapped it up with zest. "Was easy enough to beat them when I had motivation and a controlled dosage of Thanatos. Even got to such good terms with the guy who sold it to me, I distributed it for him as his muscle. Few fights later, we had desperate dope fiends with a lot of strength and no money; so, the fight game was born. Another way to take and grow."

He walked over to the table, his stomach growling as he clutched it. The thick yellow aura was growing around his body.

"I began to crave food. It started out simple enough, get takeaway, or an extra meal prep. But then my stomach started rejecting it, refusing all but one thing that rested at my feet with every fight. Flesh…" His eyes grew wide and manic, pupils enlarging before he coughed and reached under the table for another helping of some poor person's still warm corpse. "I made 'em sign a contract with me before fighting that not only was it to the death, but I could take whatever I wanted if I won. Desperate little cunts were all too eager to sign themselves away. Few choice shots to vital organs, they'd go down and be in that beautiful state between this world and the next. Unable to fight back but heart still pumping hot blood out. Delicious."

"And one of those bodies became your undoing, I assume?" I pressed, but he held a hand up.

"Not your turn. Tell me what was on that paper." He said it so matter-of-factly that the obvious nearly passed me by. "But that was… how did you…" I breathed. He seemed willing to permit this surprise as he leaned forward and pulled something from his plate, holding it up to my face.

A black feather.

"A little birdy told me. Seems he was watching you from afar to protect you. When he heard his papa was here, he went on ahead to protect him and got caught. I tell you, not a big fan of chicken, but I'll go off-menu once in a while!" He bellowed with laughter as tears filled my eyes. "I asked you a question, Nellie. I won't let you avoid it again."

All I could picture was Edgar. His laughing, constant interruptions, rude quips and that lasting image of him curled up in Nestor's arms, softly cawing and saying "Papa" over and over. No, no, I had to press it down and push on. I had to. I had to for him.

I sighed and recited what was on the paper:

"The daughter of the high priestess brings the dawn with her and the dusk in her absence.
The cycle will ring anew at her hands.
Her offering is that of her eternal servitude to guide others.

E Dolore Magna Gloria."

The thick aura began slithering its way down Cyril's body, enrapturing his muscles and his barrel chest. The smell of sulphur and burnt lard made my eyes water, but I moved past it. I paused to catch my breath and ask the question burning in the back of my skull.

"Why did you want this to be face to face, Cyril?"

He rose up out of his seat and instead of manoeuvring to another body or exercise machine, took strides toward me and reached out an arm. A hand as big as my face came ever closer. For a moment, I thought he was going to smash me into the wall, pick me up and devour me—or worse.

Instead, his large digits brushed the side of my face and his deadened eyes glazed over, a soft smile covering his face.

"Because I wanted to prove to you that I can always get what I want. One way or another." His fingers found their way to my throat and tightened around it with ease, veins pumping in his wrist as he lifted me off the ground with barely any effort. I was seeing spots within seconds, his blurry expression changing back to that of pure malice and hunger.

"Do you fear me, Nellie?" His voice cooed. This close, I could see the aura undulating around him, shaking to the very touch. I blinked twice and tried to nod, barely able to make any proper movements save for the errant kicking of my legs, desperate to find footing.

He smiled and dropped me in a heap. I gasped for air and felt my windpipe against the wall of my throat. He'd definitely considered just killing me there and then. He took his seat and looked at something behind me.

"Looks like it's almost time. Last question, Nellie. Make it a good one."

I thought about what he'd told me, how he'd gotten injured, the drug abuse and eventual supply, fighting and devouring pieces of his opponents… then I remembered something on the paper the warden gave me. Something that turned my stomach.

"What happened the night you were captured, Cyril? They say you were naught but skin and bones, shaking and convulsing from the drug. You must have gotten to this size in here, no? Tell me how you came to be one of the most feared men in this prison."

I was shaking, adrenaline pumping through me, terrified out of my mind as neurons fired to think of other ways to stall or escape. This was it. I had to stick to it.

Monks seemed to consider my question, looking down at his hands and frowning before getting up and pacing the far corner.

"I'd grown accustomed to taking pieces of my trophies home. What wasn't offered to Adephagia in that drug fuelled realm was kept for my own enjoyment. But I needed to find a more efficient way of eating at home. My wife was becoming suspicious of my constant eating out and I hoped by bringing them into that world, they'd accept it and see the good it did me. So, I offered to cook one evening for the whole family. I prepared a whole spread just to show my love and appreciation. They ate it all with relish, and said it was succulent meat. I was overjoyed. So much so that I told them what it was there and then." He turned back to me, genuine sadness in his eyes. "Things didn't go as planned. My wife lost her senses, began screaming about how I wasn't the kind, considerate, and driven man I was before the accident. How she couldn't recognise me anymore and that she was leaving. When she said she needed some space with the kids, I gave it to her. Went upstairs to think—I knew she couldn't very well tell the police anything that'd implicate her and risk losing the kids."

He stopped pacing, shoulders heaving under the weight of his words.

"I must've been on a comedown from Thanatos because I passed out and saw Adephagia again, laughing at me. Each of the mouths on her stomach and tail laughing in kind, mocking me, and biting at my torn muscles. When I woke up, I saw smoke in the house. Following it to the garage, my wife and children were in the car, eyes open and staring into the ether… dead. She'd left four words on a furiously scribbled note in the kitchen: 'Never forgive. Never forget.'"

He sighed and shook his head, pinching his nose.

"I tried to OD on Thanatos that night. I stood before Adephagia with no tributes left and no more ways to climb those hallowed steps. She looked at me with pity and said when I awoke, I'd have a new purpose. I'd capture and kill the greatest warrior I'd ever face: Nelle fucking Lockwood. So here we are, at the end of it all. No more sins for you to speak with. I'm your last stop."

He walked toward me. The surrounding aura was nearly fully over his body and I was out of time.

That's when a thought hit me.

"You ate Edgar, didn't you, Mr. Monks? Swallowed him whole with no further thought?" I couldn't help but feel a smile ripple across my face. He stopped, dumbfounded.

"I told you that already, Nellie. I also told you no more questions, so you'll have the pleasure of seeing more suffering before it's over." He made a beeline for Buck when I burst out laughing. It was a genuine, elated laugh that comes after you find something you lost and the anger, grief, and anxiety gives way.

"You stupid man. You really think he's dead, don't you? That the things you eat disappear and you don't have to deal with them anymore? God, I'm so foolish for not even realising it sooner!" I laughed harder, tears in my eyes. His face fell and lips parted to show gritted teeth.

"What the fuck do you know, eh? I've taken this meeting where I wanted it to go. I will have your flesh before this is all said and done. What does it matter if he's alive or dead?"

"It matters plenty, Mr. Monks. You ate a creature in servitude to Lady Death. You ate something that, while innocuous, is not from this world. He's pernicious, irritating, rude, and at times downright a pain in my ass—but he is a member of this group and full of many surprises. I'd also wager he's very, *very* hungry right now. I'm surprised you haven't felt him rummaging around in there, to be honest! But you will when I call out his name."

I felt a surge of power and malice run through me, as if I had the whole world in my hands. I took confident steps in front of his towering mass of muscle and saw him grow pale, shaking hands clutching at his stomach as it began to twist and gurgle.

"Edgar. Allan. Crow." I bellowed, watching this powerful man double over in agony on the floor at the mere mention, pained moans coming from his mouth as he bent over. "I'll never forgive Nestor for giving him that fucking name…" I hissed under my breath, walking round Cyril like a lioness in front of her prey.

"Pl-please… not like this." He whimpered, drool running down his beard, mingled with blood. Whatever Edgar was doing, it was efficient. I pulled him up by his beard to look at me, ushering him to lean back onto his knees and laying my hand on his face, the exact same way he did to me.

"You know what they call a flock of crows, Mr. Cyril?" I asked, moving my hand behind his head as my other pulled my serrated blade from my belt, driving it into the left of his belly and drawing it across the length with a powerful swipe.

"They call it a murder." I replied, the stench of his stomach horrifying as Edgar flew out, covered in all manner of giblets and blood, cawing as he soared around the building.

"MURDER. MURDER FAT MAN. PAPA'S BOY LIVES." He screeched, laughing as he flew to Nestor's side, cawing softly at his unconscious body.

The aura covering Cyril glowed brighter and sank into his flesh, the body shrinking and losing muscle mass before my eyes. Within a few minutes, he was scarcely anything but a skeletal frame with his stomach torn open.

Sitting back at the table within a stone's throw of him was a plate of chicken wings, Aberdeen angus steak, sausages, beans, eggs, toast, and bacon waiting for me. I knew there was no trick, no rotting food or human substitute this time. Just pure, delicious, carnivorous food. I was going to savour it.

I took my first bite, and the sound of a screaming pig filled the room. Raw and visceral, it was enough to shake anyone to their core, but my resolve was strong. I relished every bite and as I made my way through the breakfast, each new bite adding a scream to the choir of suffering creatures.

I looked straight ahead the entire time, ignoring the sound of Cyril crawling toward me and begging, weakly, for a morsel of food or another shot of Thanatos.

Only when his hand touched my thigh did I look at him, mid-bite of a sausage.

"I need… I need to see her again. I know how this works, you see my sin in physical form and I go with them to ascend… you can't get rid of me until then… Please…" His eyes were sinking into his gaunt face, his beard now brittle and patchy, teeth yellowing and falling out. I scoffed and bit down hard on the sausage, the juices spraying in front of him.

"Your sin was so powerful, so full of desire, that it manifested around you and ate itself. You didn't wonder why you ballooned up and deflated so quick? You are the ouroboros, Mr. Monks. You feed upon yourself in the end. Or, perhaps, there's a better way to say this—let me think…" I turned away again and saw Edgar watching me, head cocked to the side and undoubtedly observing the best tactic to steal from me. I pulled a piece of my egg away and threw it into Cyril's open cavity.

As expected, he dove straight in, rummaging up through Cyril's organs and causing him ungodly damage and pain in the process.

But after the way he'd toyed with me, used information against me, and put my loved ones through hell, I was unfazed. Perhaps I had ascended in my own way, grown a tad. I also knew the warden was watching. I wanted him to see that I was no longer going to play any games. Not for our last two sins.

This whole prison would know not to fuck with Nelle Lockwood.

As I finished my last few bites and the death rattles of Cyril Monks faded with the agonised screams of the animals I'd eaten, I made sure he heard one last prophetic phrase before he left this world. Getting out of my seat, I stood over him on my way to rescue my friends.

"That which is gluttonous may eternal lie. And even in strange aeons, even you may die."

-

Inmate: *#5933: Cyril Monks*
Sin: *Gluttony*
Food: *A full English breakfast, complete with the screams of those we devour.*

The Sixth Sin: Ira (Wrath)

Just two sins stood between us and the end of our time in this dismal prison.

I stared at the body of Cyril Monks, my meal complete and malice still surging through my veins. I could still see, feel, and sense his sins. Every fabric of my being wanted so badly to hurt him further. I had an inescapable desire to sink my teeth into his face and bite off his nose—an urge so strong that I felt it well up in me and stopped, gritting my teeth.

It was Nestor's laboured breathing and cries of pain at seeing Buck that pulled me from that lapse in moral judgment. He called out and before I could even step ahead, the doors flung open and droves of the warden's men flooded the room, cordoning off the area and tending to a still unconscious Buck.

"Well, you certainly proved you know your stuff, Frau Lockwood." The warden stood by the body of Cyril, looking down at him and tutting. "I did not expect you to get... physical with him. Aber, this is the person you are becoming. Perhaps this prison is the right place for you after all, ja?" He jested, but his eyes were full of curiosity and a spot of what appeared to be joy.

"I did what I had to do, nothing more. But I'd like to rest before I take on the next inmate, if you please." I flatly replied, adrenaline steadily wearing off and fatigue setting in. He stood up and cracked his neck, shrugging his shoulders and rolling up his sleeves.

"Des Teufels liebstes Möbelstück ist die lange Bank." He replied, shaking his head before looking at me and clarifying in English. "The devil's favourite piece of furniture is the bench. What you put off now for later allows the devil to win. Better to at least get it done sooner, rather than later. Besides, this inmate is different. #0744 is a unique one that will take even you by surprise, I think. His name is Eldon Calico. Thirty-six years old. You will have no trouble ascertaining what you need in record time, of that I assure you. In fact..." He walked over to Nestor and inspected his wound, physicians attending to him as the others put Buck on a stretcher and extracted him from the room in a hurry. "Mit Herr Holden and das... Krähe Edgar with you, I don't think you'll even need my information. This will be a test of only your patience."

I opened my mouth to protest, but what use was there in arguing with a megalomaniac? I simply sighed and made my way for the door.

"How long will Buck's surgery be?" I asked, hoping to at least give myself some time to nap and eat. The food of the sins I ingested never filled me.

"I'd say six hours, if we're quick. Use that time to finish this sin and rest up. I assure you that you'll be out within the hour. Grab something from the green room to eat and we'll patch up Herr Holden. You have twenty minutes." He saw the discontent in my face and his expression softened. "I am testing you only because I believe in your abilities, Frau Lockwood. You are the bright star in this prison and I'm so proud of you."

With nothing else to say, I turned on my heel and took the long journey to the green room.

I'm not so proud I can't admit that when the door finally closed, my body slumped against the back wall and I burst into tears, pulling my knees up to my chest as I sobbed.

I failed them both. I was brash; I made mistakes, and it cost them both. Oh, Buck...

Within a few minutes of self pitying, the elevator stopped and the green room was in sight. My knees struggled to hold my frame up as I swayed from side to side, praying for sustenance that would provide some kind of boost.

A pot of coffee on, and some sandwiches in my system, I slumped into the chair and felt my eyes flutter, if for a moment.

Darkness enveloped me. Flashes of images from my past: the smell of my mum's cooking, her begging me to stay indoors, the cool summer air and thick brambles scratching my arms as I rushed toward an unholy light in the distance, a man with wide eyes beckoning to me... a struggle. Blood. Searing pain.

Then, the figure standing in a fire pit. His body scorched, chunks of his flesh melting and plopping onto the floor. Rickety arms reached out in front of me and held up one finger each, his smile drooping into a frown as muscle tissue struggled to hold his lips together when the heat spread over his body.

Two.

I snapped up. The pot of coffee was boiled and it looked like I'd been out for a few minutes. Downing the coffee and getting changed in the restroom, I took a leap of faith and grabbed for the totem in my pocket, hoping I'd simply had a lapse in judgment and it was perfectly fine.

Instead, it was segmented into three distinct pieces. My eyes burned at the mere sight of it in that state.

If it weren't for Nestor shouting at Edgar in the hallway, I'm sure my anxiety would've overtaken me.

"Damnit Edgar, stop preening over my wound, it's fine!" Nestor bellowed between intermittent "OW""s as Edgar flew around and cawed softly.

"Help, Papa. Eat Dead Flesh. Helps Edgar." He cackled, flying toward me and nuzzling against my neck as he landed on my shoulder, clearly trying to curry favour with me. I had to admit, it was working.

"It's not dead flesh!" Nestor protested, rubbing the sore wound and grabbing himself a drink. "Miss Lockwo—Er, Nelle, we'll head up in a minute. You just keep that idiot son of mine busy so he doesn't try nibbling at my flesh, okay?" He sighed and walked into the green room.

"All flesh dead flesh." Edgar softly quipped before repeating "Papa" over and over as I stroked him and felt a weak smile run across my face for the first time in so long.

A moment of clarity I would come to appreciate and yearn for in time.

-

As we stepped out into the visitation area, the guard saw us through and pointed us to the farthest room on the end, a large circular dome of sorts that on first inspection would be mistaken for an IKEA showroom—furniture that had never been touched, sat upon, or utilised in any way was strewn about the place. A bookcase with nothing adorning it, a dining table that had makeshift plates and silverware, but no food. It was entirely bizarre and sat in the centre of it all was a meek man, perched on a chair with his hands nervously running over his well-ironed trousers and occasionally fiddling with the collar of his shirt as furtive eyes met ours. He got up with a wide, sincere smile and unwavering politeness.

"Ah, you must be Madame Lockwood? A pleasure, I'm Eldon. I'm sure you're tired, so I'll try not to take much of your time." He outstretched a shaking hand, and I simply stared at it, the smell rushing through my nostrils but not enough to place its designated scent or reminiscent taste. He retracted the hand and rocked on his feet. "Of course, probably not wise to touch me; I am an inmate here, after all. Shall we?"

Nestor and Edgar took their spot nearby, Edgar teasing Eldon from afar, much to Nestor's chagrin.

"FLANDERS. SMELLS LIKE SULPHUR."

If Eldon took offence, he didn't show it as we took our seats on opposing sides of the dining table. I saw something moving in the dome, but I kept my focus on Eldon.

"So, Mr. Calico, why are you in here?" I asked, watching his body language closely. "If you don't mind me saying; you're a little different from our usual clientele. Was there a mix up?"

This seemed to relax him, and he let out a hearty laugh. Perfect white teeth shimmered in the light, giving him an almost holy visage.

"Ah, well, we all have our sins and our troubles, do we not? I've made some mistakes, maybe upset a few people with my temper, but I'm much better now. It's a credit to this facility, and hopefully to you for being able to take the remnants of those past-life sins from me."

That smell was beginning to grow unbearable, and the surrounding pressure was growing heavy. I looked to Nestor before sighing and turning my attention back to Eldon.

"Do you like children, Eldon?" I asked, feeling my knuckles grow white from the clenching of my fists. He cocked his head to the side and gave a sincere grin, kind eyes softly resting on me.

"Of course. I would distrust anyone who didn't enjoy their free spirits and open kindness." He leaned back and rested his hands in his lap. "They are the future, truly. What other kind of answer is there?"

I took a deep breath in and held it in my lungs, letting the smell of sulphur burn inside me before I exhaled and felt the burning on my tongue.

"Do you like fucking them?" I asked it as bluntly as one could do. Letting the moment hang in the air as I wished his fetid body to do. His smile was the first to fade; it twitched and resisted as the corners were dragged down and the glimmering teeth shut off from my view. I persisted. "You must, since you continued doing it even after your community found out and excommunicated you instead of calling the police since the parents didn't want to press charges. You ensured that frightened girl was the first of so, so many."

His aura was steeped in tar and trudged about the place, its stain marking every single section of the furniture it touched in countless hand prints, searing hot to the touch and full of unspeakable foul odours and liquids. The furniture only looked pristine on the outside, but once you got closer…

"That's your core fault, but not what put you here, is it, Mr. Calico? No, it's what you did upon the knowledge the town was gathering evidence to put you away, to stop you seeing the child you fathered with one of those little girls. Because they *were* little girls, Eldon. You just got to one of them after puberty, you fucking animal." I was finding it harder and harder to keep my cool. I could see exactly why the warden was testing me.

He knew I'd sense the man out before I even spoke to him.

Eldon's eyes seemed to sink into his skull, pupils dilating and losing the bright hue they'd once possessed. He stood up from the table slowly and began breathing heavily, shoulders hunching as veins appeared on his neck. Still, I persisted.

"You got angry—so angry, in fact, that you tore them apart with your bare hands and teeth, one by one. Twenty villagers all massacred by your hand, including your own child. One swing and you silenced his cries. You arrive here, you think you find god or whatever the fuck this whole nice guy act is… and you think you can pull the wool over anyone's eyes, even mine." I stood up and walked across to face him, some odd fifteen feet separating us. "Well, it took me nine minutes to figure out your shit and I already know your sin. Y'know, wrath may be one of the oldest sins, but my god, is it easy to spot."

The plate on my table started to fill, a blowfish finely cut with all the wrong parts waiting to be devoured. Eldon's breathing gave way to growls and grunts as his muscles grew and ripped his shirt, eyes growing vacant.

"SHUT UP. YOU KNOW NOTHING OF WHO I AM!" Fists smashed the table as I dove for the plate, finding cover and eating it as quick as I could. Eldon tore furniture to bits as Nestor stepped in and Edgar flew overhead, rushing in to peck at his face before flitting away.

I felt the poisonous rage fill my body almost instantly, hot anger of the prior sins, interactions with the warden, with this fucking monstrosity in front of me. I no longer cared to see him eaten by a tulpa, whatever that sludge addled creature was. I wanted him dead by *my* hand.

My vision shook as I rose from my spot, knife drawn as I waited for a chance to mount his back and began driving my serrated blade into his soft flesh. Finding a soft area on his shoulder blade, I drove it in to the hilt before pulling on it with all my body weight, splitting the flesh.

He was screaming. Good. I wanted him in pain; I wanted him upset. I issued a boot to the face for good measure while he howled and bled onto the floor.

The sludge tulpa ferried its way over to where Eldon sat, peering over at him curiously. But I wasn't done. Another boot to the face knocked him onto his back. I stood over him, my heart beating fast, and wrath coursing through my body. I drove the knife straight into his groin with a screech I did not think I'd ever produce. Nestor simply stared in horror and Edgar cried out "NOPE."

Eldon's cries of pain were music to my ears as the sludge tulpa sank over him and drowned out any notion of his anger, his pain, and his protests. As though he was being smothered, he fought back with extreme prejudice until the life steadily left him and he was nothing more than a stuck pig on the ground.

"You weren't worth a proper conversation or anything close to it." I spat on his body before walking straight for the door, not even wanting to look back or stomach the smell of his sin any longer. "We good, Nestor?"

Nestor shuffled and cleared his throat, knowing I was making my way for the infirmary to see Buck.

"Yeah… yeah, we're good. Guess it's time to be thankful whatever you ate doesn't last too long…"

Buck was still out cold when I got to the infirmary, his body wracked with cuts and bruises. I was told his hand wasn't salvageable and instead he'd be given a state-of-the-art prosthetic. I don't know how they did it, but this damn thing could actually flex and respond in the same way his flesh counterpart did.

Seeing him like this, so damaged and hurt… I felt the blame overwhelm my wrath the moment I stepped near his bed.

Eyes fluttering and gently opening to see me, that smile that could melt the ice caps still prevalent in spite of his injuries.

"Always a pleasure, Nelle. I take it you stopped that big bastard?" He paused, and I simply nodded, hand caressing his tired face.

"We ran into some trouble up there with ya, Buck. Had some complications that required us to go on without you. Wasn't personal, just had to be done." Nestor shuffled, clearly not used to giving bedside words of comfort. "But you needed to heal, y'see."

"Heal? From some bumps and scra—oh… oh, I see…" His voice fell to a croaky whisper of affirmation as he flexed his hand and mechanical fingers responded in kind. For a moment I thought rage, misery, or despair would take him. But instead, he laughed. "Well, I knew I'd lose something vital in this job sooner or later! I'm lucky I got as far as I did, to be honest… and hey, now I got a badass fist to punch with and not worry about medical bills after!" He laughed, and I felt my heart swell to bursting.

I did this. I put him here.

"We've got one inmate left to go, a whole day to rest up, and then we'll be heading on over to it. Think you're up to the task?" Nestor leaned in and Edgar hopped off of his shoulder and onto Buck's bed, looking up at him and cocking his head.

"ROBOCOP. METALMAN. EVEN COOLER." he cawed as Buck gently patted his head, smiling.

"I'm the last and best McGraw they have, I can't very well expand the compendium from a hospital bed, can I? Let's get this bad boy calibrated and then get moving."

I pulled the heavy book out of my bag and dropped it on his lap with an audible "oof." I smiled and broke into a chuckle.

"Look on the bright side, Buck. You didn't lose your writing hand!"

We laughed, and it felt like the last few days were nothing short of a bad dream or a distant memory. But we knew we had one final sin to go and that it would be the largest obstacle to climb.

No warden in sight, no prophetic illusions, just the knowledge we were moving ahead.

As Buck opened the compendium, a dossier slipped out and fell to the side. Curious, we looked at it and saw the title on top:

Prisoner Inmate #001.

Opening it up brought more pain and sorrow than anything I could have been prepared for.

Not because of the crimes they'd committed, of which there were countless.

Not because of their sin or their tulpa, of which there was almost no info save for the sin of "Pride."

But because of the name and photo attached, the name and photo that I have burned into my brain for over a decade.

The photo was of a dishevelled woman in her fifties, dead in the eyes, and a smug grin stretched across her face, bearing the sigil of The Church of the Duskwalker.

Her name? Gwenllian Nia Lockwood

"Mum…"

-

Inmate #0744: *Eldon Calico, The Beast of Felixstowe.*
Sin: *Wrath*
Food: *A blowfish filled with a poisonous rage that would infect and harm oneself as much as it did others.*

The Seventh Sin: Superbia (Pride)

I've just eviscerated the vile man who represented wrath. Now, I am tasked with the final sin. The significance of that person is not lost on me.

My own mother.

"How… how is this… I don't…" I couldn't find the words as my mind struggled to comprehend what I was seeing. The sounds of Buck and Nestor calling after me faded to nothing as I fainted, exhaustion and anxiety crippling my ability to function.

This time, when dreams took hold, I saw a series of rooms. Some of them small and familiar, others big, foreboding and alien to me. But I occupied them all, sometimes on my own and other times with friends, lovers, family.

In every single instance, that spectre was right behind me. Sometimes looming overhead as bad news was handed down, perching in the corners of the room to observe me carefully as I did something innocuous. No matter where I went in these various rooms of my life, it was always close by, as if attached to me.

Even as the scene shifted to this prison, it occupied the same spaces we did. Standing in the corner during lust's interrogation, off to the side for greed, directly overhead for envy, under the table for sloth, holding onto me for gluttony, and cowering behind a table for wrath.

My mind was directed to the green room where my body now lay, in a moment of lucid dreaming. I watched as this abomination crawled over my sleeping frame and held a single digit up, before cracking its head at me and rushing toward me, the smile ever present on its decaying face:

One.

I didn't snap awake as before. I'd come to expect the terrors my sleeping world brought. Instead, I breathed deep and looked around. I saw Edgar had nestled himself in my hair, sleeping softly.

"Comfy. Mama. Safe." He softly chirped, flattering me as I smiled and looked over at Nestor, reading a book and rolling his eyes.

"Don't be expecting marriage now, Miss Lockwood. You're already spoken for. Wouldn't be appropriate." He shot a sly grin my way and noted the clock. "You've been out for a while. Buck is just getting changed and we'll head on up as soon as you're ready."

"Have you heard from Warden Leichenberg? He's usually around when I wake up. I'd like to have a word with him about these tests." I tried not to grit my teeth as I reciprocated his smile.

"Do these words involve fists and or feet hurtling toward his body?" Nestor asked, feigning concern as he shut his book and went over to the fridge to fetch me some food. I gently got up and scooped Edgar into my hands.

"Perhaps. But a lady doesn't kick and tell." I slyly replied, breaking into a laugh and trying to force the job to the back of my mind.

"Well, no. He was dealing with the fallout of Cyril Monks' breakout and some other issues. Since it's Prisoner #001, there's a lot of other logistical things he says he's gotta do. But, he did tell me that he'd meet us at their cell." Nestor shut the fridge and handed me some sandwiches and a glass of orange juice. "Now eat up, we've got way better food on the plane."

"Mind if I ask you something, Nestor?" I bit into the cheese and ham sandwiches with joy, my stomach grateful for a proper meal. He nodded and gestured for me to continue. "What's it like working for Lady Death?"

He paused and thought for a moment, finding the right way to say something about someone who I can only assume was always listening in.

"No day is the same, no night is dull. She has a saying that I've tried to take with me into life, especially on difficult jobs that I know will entail a lot of pain, struggle, and heartache." He cleared his throat. "It takes courage to accept one's fate, bravery to step beyond the threshold, and sincerity to see it for what it is. Death can be as foreboding or as forgiving as you make it. It is a journey we must all undertake and though we walk it on our own, it does not need to be without loving company at the end."

"Cheesy, but I like it. It's certainly a motto to live by." Edgar began to wake up and, upon seeing my food, gently preened me until I gave him some. He was being so adorable that it was hard to resist.

"We had some trouble with our own terrorist group a while ago. They called themselves The Mortal Coil and attached to the bodies of the recently deceased. Said that death itself was a crime against humanity and needed to be stopped. When we dealt with them, it meant dealing with uncomfortable conversations about life, death, and everything in between. At the end of it all, it made me realise something..." He trailed off, lips trembling as the door opened and Buck walked in, buttoning his shirt and still fumbling with his bionic hand.

"It taught ya that all moments matter and we should take life by the horns and hold on until it bucks us off?" Buck smiled, laughing despite his low energy, still making my heart skip a beat. "I'm glad you're up, Nelle. Ready to beat this thing and go home?"

I tried to smile, to feign confidence, but the moment he mentioned the job at hand, I felt my face fall.

"Hey, Nellie. You know that whatever is in there, it's beatable. If it *is* your mother, we can still deal with this properly. Nobody has to get hurt if we don't want them to, but..." He kneeled down and looked me in the eyes, a melancholy twinkling in the corners I'd seldom seen. "I'm not sure that's your mother. I think someone has been playing a long, long game at our expense."

I thought about what he said. The tests, the visions, the information the inmates had. It started to fit together like a jigsaw puzzle that filled me with a disgust and anger not dissimilar to that for envy, gluttony, or wrath.

"Why? Why would they do this? More importantly, who?" As I asked, Buck stood up and stared straight at the camera, anger strewn across his face as brows furrowed.

"Oh, I'd imagine the same person who put that dossier in my book. But it's just a hunch—a 'test' if you will. But, we're losing time and our last inmate awaits. I'm sure we'll know who this is when the job is done."

"I reckon you're right, may as well finish the job together. Not much else to do until then. But I'm sure we'll still have an ass to kick when all's said and done, right, Edgar?"

"BEATING TIME. BEATING TIME." He flapped his wings and circled around the room before hopping over to Nestor's shoulder. We made for the elevator and the attending guard took us down to the gen pop area.

"They've put all the inmates into their cells, giving you the space with inmate #001. Warden says that you may need the extra room and the inmates would be a distraction." The guard pointed out the window as we carried on descending, the huge hole in the back wall sending out foreboding sensations even from this distance.

"Fine, makes the job easier. We'll be sure to thank him." I quipped, checking over my equipment as the elevator came to a stop and we made our way across the expansive threshold to the wall. As I looked at the several stories of cells around us, I could feel the collective murderous intent of thousands of inmates bearing down on us.

It felt so much as if we were the caged animals they were observing for our enjoyment.

The closer we got, the more the smell hit my nostrils and the more my emotions bubbled to the surface.

It was the smell of her cooking. Almost exactly as I remembered it from so many years ago.

"Nelle, no matter what you see in there, I need you to keep professional, okay?" Buck's voice cut through the lapse in focus, and he took my hand in his. "I know what you're going to feel in there, what you might see, but at all times, keep your wits about you. That could be the difference between life and death. And no matter what, we'll be here for you."

I smiled and nodded. He was always a good tutor and instilled me with that additional sliver of confidence I didn't know I had. When we approached the threshold, I saw the warm glow from the large cell and a voice call out:

"Just you, my love. The boys will need to wait outside!"

My ears must have been malfunctioning. It sounded *just* like her.

"M-mum? Is that you?" A redundant question, I know, but everything in that moment was surreal.

"Well, I don't recall changing my name recently, so yes, it's Mum. Are you coming in?"

I looked at Buck, Nestor, and Edgar, all of whom looked a mixture of confused and concerned as they shrugged and nodded to the opening.

Taking a deep breath, I stepped over the threshold.

—

Once inside, the cell was a total remake of our old home. Small handmade decorations lined the walls, photos of my family and I adorned the main shelves, and over a makeshift kitchen stood my mother. Nothing like her mugshot, she'd not aged a day since I last saw her. She was tall, voluptuous and beautiful, her large afro now tucked into a braided beehive, still sporting blue overalls and a cheesy apron as she hummed softly while cooking.

It was almost too much to bear.

"Sit down, love. I'll be with you in a minute. I'm sure you have lots of questions!" Her calming voice soothed me so that I did as she instructed without question. I planted myself on a comfortable leather sofa, awkwardly ensuring my weapons weren't hidden or obstructed. I watched as the woman I'd not seen in over a decade turned and that warm, beautiful smile met my own, setting down some tea in front of us.

"Food will be a while, so I thought tea would be sufficient. Oh, oh my..." She looked over at me and truly saw me, eyes filling with tears as she reached for a handkerchief. "Eleanor... my Nelle... all grown up. You're beautiful."

I smiled and tried my best to hide the tears, albeit in vain as they fell down my face.

"Mum, I've missed you so much. But, I have to know..." I felt my stomach tie into knots as I started, but her warm smile and nodding helped ground me.

"I know you do, love. You need to know how I got here, how this is going to go, and what will happen next. I suppose we should start with the first question, yeah?"

I nodded and took a sip of the tea. Earl Grey with a hint of honey, her own little blend that took me right back to home. I'd tried for so many years to replicate it, unsuccessfully.

"That night, I got radioed that there was someone in the middle of the new forest. They'd been seen starting a fire, and obviously it was my job to investigate. Initially, I thought it was just a usual disturbance. Kids being kids and all that, but I saw the colour from the treeline and I knew it was something else. Someone was calling me to them."

I thought back to what DeSantos had mentioned, that Mum was Mother Accumulator, Head Priestess of The Church of the Duskwalkers.

"Mum, I was told you were involved in a church, one that I wasn't aware of. Is this true?" Again, the anxiety mounted. I didn't want to know these things of my own mother were true, but the necessity of asking is why I am here. Her face fell, and she looked ashamed.

"When I joined them, it wasn't what it grew to be. The All Father who ran it was an astoundingly brilliant man rife with ideas of how the world could be. He wanted to bring about great change and saw opportunities in his beliefs. When I helped him, I was merely a sort of spiritual advisor. As we Lockwoods can see things others can't, that was my main point for being there. But it grew into something worse. When I tried to leave, he told me he'd take you. The pride of his convent. That's who was waiting for me in the forest clearing that night."

The smell of her cooking grew stronger, mixing with other scents I didn't immediately recognise. There were some discussions outside, but I wasn't focused on them.

"What happened in the forest? I remember seeing something in my dreams, but I know when I woke up, I was in the cabin…" I struggled to find the words, as if it was confusing me to put the events together. She shook her head.

"No, after I got to the clearing and saw the All Father there, standing in the middle of a fire pit, a strange black void to his left… I knew something was wrong. He told me that it was time to introduce you to the church properly. I told him you weren't ready, that I wanted to give you the option of choice. Sweetheart, when you tell a man as proud as that that he cannot have something, it doesn't end well. You must have seen the lights or heard the commotion because right as he began walking for the house and I struggled with him, out you came looking confused and terrified."

Mum looked forlorn and genuinely afraid as she spoke. "Nelle, looking upon the All Father without prior preparations is often too much for anyone, let alone an adolescent. You screamed, and he made a grab for you, trying to extract what he wanted. My instincts kicked in and I snatched you away, holding you as your consciousness flittered. That's where my pride comes in, and he…"

Her eyes filled with tears and she covered her shame with her hands as she sobbed. It was a bizarre moment, seeing your still young mother sobbing in front of you. It's not something you're often used to dealing with.

"Mum, I'm sure you did everything you could to protect me. No matter what you did, I'll still love you." I soothed her, not having the confidence to reach out, but still wanting to assure her.

"But that's just it, Nelle. I made a grave mistake. I let him take you." She looked up at me, eyes red and full of pain. "He spoke in my ear of things to come if you were brought into the church, to his influence, and I let him infect you with his pride as he had done me. You writhed, screamed, and after some time… fell silent. When you woke up, I was trying to tend to you and I saw the rage in your eyes. The betrayal. You pushed me back and… and I fell through."

There was a silence that hung heavy in the air. It felt like my mind was splitting under the weight of what I was being told. Hot flashes of that night rushing through my mind, no man in them save for a pair of malicious eyes and a wide grin bearing down on me.

Not dissimilar to the one from my nightmares.

"I fell into the void and felt every atom of myself disintegrate, Nelle. I died over and over in that black stygian void. Then, I awoke and was brought here by the warden. He made me comfortable and told me I was sentenced to death, by my own daughter. The Last Sin Eater." She finished and smiled weakly at me, grief and acceptance bearing down on me. "I am at peace with what comes next. Which leads me onto your next question."

"Stygian void… how did you…" I began, but she shook her head and drank more of her tea.

"What happens next, is you take that knife in your holster and you do what needs to be done. You end things here and now. You let your mother go to her eternal rest, knowing she confessed her sin." She stared at me, utmost sincerity in her eyes. "You do the job Grandma and Grandpa trained you for, and you do what needs to be done after."

Even when asking for death, she carried grace and beauty with her, sipping her tea and getting up to wash the cup. She looked at me as she wrung her hands, my mouth still hanging open.

"No matter what happens, you will always be my daughter. You will always be Nelle Lockwood. You carry that name with pride." She walked over to a little speaker dock that housed the iPod she would one day give me, clicking play. "You never forget that for all the errors and mistakes we make, we Lockwoods are good at our core." She breathed in, not looking at me as she carried on washing up. "I'm ready to go home, Nellie…"

The high hats began ringing out and the soft dulcet tones of Sam Carter filled my ears. She certainly had a knack for choosing appropriate music, even if it was breaking my heart in the process.

"There must be an easier way to release these feelings."

I stood up, drawing my knife and taking shaky steps toward my mother.

"So far from home, I need your voice to hold my head together."

I just needed to aim for between the ribs, strike with all my power, and pierce her heart in one motion. It would be over within moments.

"So... So far from home, I need your voice to lift my lonely state of mind."

I pulled the hilt around and gripped it, feeling every nerve in my hand tense up as it had done so many times before. The smell of her cooking overwhelmed me.

Visions of her buying me my first animal book for Christmas, me dressing up as her for school as my hero. Stop it. Stop it. Please.

"Oh, there must be an easier way."

It would be over within moments.

"Oh, there must be an easier way. To release these feelings."

I stepped closer, grabbing her shoulder with my left, spinning her around and driving the knife in with my right. Her body let out a gasp of air and eyes were wide, but a smile was written across her face. She relaxed and fell forward, arms draped around my body.

"I will always be with you. Always in those places when you're at your lowest. I love you, Nelle."

I laid her body down, closing her eyes, and sobbed over her body.

I wish I could tell you that this is the end of my tale. That we excised the last sinner from this prison, packed up and left. That I mourned my mother's loss and gave her a beautiful send off.

But that is rarely the way these sorts of things go.

The lights shut off, and we were bathed in a dark red light as the warden's voice boomed over the intercom.

"I see you vanquished the last sin, your own mother... bravo, Frau Lockwood. You exceeded all my expectations and I must say..." His voice dropped, the German accent lifted, and a powerful accent not dissimilar to my own British cadence rang out. "I am so *proud* of you. I think it might be time to put an end to this, don't you?"

I felt my head burn, looking down at the body of my mother and realising that not only was there no blood on my person, but there was none on her either. She glowed with a bright white aura and the smell of her cooking gave way as she faded in front of me. The room I stood in was now barren and filthy. Outside, I heard Buck and Nestor scuffling and upon stepping outside, saw Buck standing over Nestor with his hand firmly clenched around something broken in his pocket.

The totems we'd been given, destroyed.

"I went ahead and ensured that there were no extra... issues in my release from this place. Pride lives not only in you, Miss Lockwood, but in Mr. McGraw as well... I took some extra liberties when he was being operated upon."

An alarm rang out and the horrifying sounds of every cell door opening filled the once silent prison halls, the main doors giving way as figures began to pile in. Familiar figures.

"You thought that you were absolving these evildoers, sending them to their gods and resigning them to whatever fates befell them. But no, you were the key to freeing them of their mortal coils and allowing them to go back to the forms they once housed. My situation is a little more complex. You may have gotten rid of pride, but I am something *more* than pride. But you know that all too well, don't you?"

The visages of an incubus, Mammon, Moloch, Cirke, Belphegor, Adi, and the sludge Tulpa burst through the doors as inmates stand over the railings looking at us.

"Like father, like daughter." His guttural laughter filled the room as dread built in my soul.

He cleared his throat and tapped the mic. Every head that wasn't previously looking toward the shrouded warden's office now craned their necks up as he spoke again.

"Attention all inmates: First prisoners to kill Nestor Holden, Edgar Crow, Sir Simon Buck Nasty McGraw, and capture Nelle Lockwood alive shall have their sentences commuted. Until then, this facility is in lockdown."

I stood at the foot of utter oblivion, not knowing where to start as violence and murderous intent rushed toward me, Buck, still in a trancelike state, and Nestor on the ground.

This truly felt like the end. The mocking intonations of the All Father rained down on me as he signed off, piercing eyes and that all too familiar grin from my nightmares bore into my skull:

"Good luck Nelle, I'm already *proud* of you."

The Final Sin: Tristitia (Despair)

"I believe that unarmed truth and unconditional love will have the final word in reality. This is why right, temporarily defeated, is stronger than evil triumphant."

Doctor King said that when facing a scenario that offered the hardest path ahead. A path that involved tackling the harshest kinds of racial injustices in order to root out the systemic issues that the nation had—still has.

I believe we can root them out together, through difficult conversations and actionable change.

My name is Madame Nelle Lockwood. I'm the Last Sin Eater. This is the end of my story.

-

I stood in that space for what felt like minutes. The tulpas of older sins now rushing at me, Nestor pinned to the ground with a still confused Buck's foot, Edgar nowhere to be seen as the droves of inmates descended from all sides, malice on their minds and hands ready to tear us apart.

To say I felt the enormity of the situation pressing upon me would be a gross understatement.

I pulled my knife out, my mind still swelling with questions on how my mother was here, only to fade to what was wrong with Buck, to the relation I had with the warden—The All Father—but I had to push forward with the task at hand: eviscerating as many of the inmates as possible.

It was only when a knife pierced my chest that I felt the world fall silent. My mouth grew hot, and I felt my breathing grow shallow, gasping for air that wasn't coming. I looked up at Buck and saw the agony in his face, as if his limbs acted without his instruction.

"Buck..." was all I managed to speak before the world grew cold and distant.

The last thing I recalled for the longest time was darkness. All I knew was a bitter, unforgiving void that enraptured the soul, froze the bones, and made my flesh feel as if it were in a charnel house. Piece after piece of me was stripped away, and my consciousness scattered in so many directions.

It felt as if I were being pulled in multiple directions at once, sensory overload interspersed with a sense of total calm. I was where I should be.

"Eleanor Gwynedd Lockwood, I've heard so much about you."

From the absolute darkness came a small, delicate flame, situated in a lantern that hung on a long thick chain attached to a great metallic pole. It jutted out from the darkness with no bearer visible. The black and white flame danced in its glass prison and the closer it came to me, the more put together I felt. My sight began to clear, my hearing returned, and the muffled voice grew in clarity, a pronounced English woman's voice that cut the air and brought familiarity. I could smell ginseng and sage on her person and felt at ease.

A body broke through, following the lantern. Cloaked in a gown of darkness, her skeletal frame reaching out to me, pulling my body upright and straight. Her face was hidden behind a mourning veil, the fragments of bone still apparent.

"You will find it difficult to speak, so until you have regained that ability, I ask you to listen. You are facing a moment that many encounter at some point in their lives. For some, it is minute and inconsequential. For others, it is a moment the world is watching them commit to. All are noted and all have reactions. You have reached your first of many, Nelle." She offered a bony hand clasped in bracelets and jewellery to me; I took it and didn't even register the issues she should be having with strength. She pulled me forward and I found myself standing on invisible ground, the surrounding light only serving to display the absolute nothingness around us until she waved her hand.

"What—am I…" I croaked, my voice still finding its footing. Her hand passed by my face and I saw the enormity of creation beneath my feet, the exact same as my nightmares. Luminous stars in beautiful patterns, nebulas passing underneath while galaxies rotate overhead.

"Dead? No. You're merely asleep. A moment, or perhaps a space, between is a better phrase. You will make a choice, you will wake up, and everything will change. Every action is a consequence." She sighed. "I just wish it hadn't gone this way. Truly, I do. This is why I don't get involved in personal matters or individual rites anymore, too messy."

She clicked her fingers and the area beneath our feet rushed forward, down to our world and eventually to Sturgeon. I saw all my friends and citizens going about their day, each one blissfully unaware that the very same sins I'd excised in the prison were now latching themselves to their bodies. The sun steadily grew darker as a great calamity wrapped around it, bathing the city in twilight.

"Should you falter here, Nelle, this is what will strike Sturgeon, what will befall every soul in due time with enough malice, rhetoric, and patience. The All Father—Amos—he will not stop. None of them will. The Unbounded shall take every soul they can until there is no more to take. Then…"

She cast her head up to the visages of the seven monstrosities obscured in the depths of the skies, eyes and mouths awash with glee as ascended humans willingly threw themselves into their gaping jaws, growing their strength. Eventually, they would form together and send a single arc of black light down to Sturgeon, obliterating it in seconds. My horror at the scene was only beaten by the grief I felt at so many lives snuffed out in an instant, a responsibility on my shoulders that I did not understand.

"Nothing. They will move to their next destination and start all over again. As they have done for countless aeons. This is what awaits them all if you are not able to make a choice. The right choice. The only choice."

"What is the offer?" I asked after a long pause. She kept her gaze on the destruction below, then looked at her hands, the light of the lantern illuminating them brilliantly.

"A life for a life. A sacrifice to put the path in the direction it needs to go in."

The scene shifted to the prison and the carnage approaching us in slow motion. To Buck, standing over a confused Nestor with his eyes glazed.

"He was infected with a pride trigger. It shifts the perspective and pushes any good soul to terrible deeds. Yours seems to be in control, but Buck is too weak after his surgery. He will kill Nestor if I do not intervene. If *you* do not intervene." She turned to me, a weariness to her voice, her black cloak shimmering with the souls of so many countless individuals waiting to be ferried to their next life.

Before I could reply, she clicked her fingers again and a series of flashing images flitted in front of me: people I'd never met but had an inexplicable and deep bond with flashed up—all of them dead. Some had smiles on their faces, some spoke of reuniting with the family they lost, missing those they left behind. Others were gone in a flash. All of them giving their lives in pursuit of a better future—a future without Amos. Without The Unbounded.

"Why am I crying? I don't know these people. I don't... I don't understand." I felt the pain rush through my body, the first true pain I'd felt since I woke here. An agony insurmountably stronger than that of the physical, as if I were reliving the loss of my mother ad infinitum.

Lady Death took my hand in hers, never taking her eyes off of the slew of bodies laying and waiting for her and her emissaries to collect them.

"You will eventually, Nelle." She said softly, her dulcet tones ringing in my ears and pulling at my heartstrings as if she shared every ounce of my grief. "You will, and you'll be so thankful for it, so much better for it. These people will one day shape you. It all starts here."

As the image snapped back to Buck, I felt myself fall into that age-old adage of bargaining, knowing full well the futility in such an act.

"Send me back with your blessing. An imbued weapon, *anything* to take them down, and I swear I can protect him. I can get to the All Father and... and maybe if I do, the pride infection in Buck will go?"

"A solemn acceptance is the hardest thing. I understand. If you feel you can, I will give you the chance—but my offer doesn't change. A life for a life. Be that All Father Amos or Buck's... it is not for me to decide." She handed me a cloth wrapped weapon and placed her hands over mine, the glow of her bracelets nearly blinding me. "This is just a dream, but you will recall everything when you awaken. This will be with you as well as my guide. Look after him, will you? He's one of my favourites." Her bony smile was still visible. I didn't know how a skull could mould its features, but I felt that overwhelming sense of comfort as I wiped the tears away and smiled.

The Last Sin Eater

Everything grew blurry and my body began to ache once more, my chest throbbing and burning as the scene cleared and faded from view.

"Thank you, my lady."

-

The cold floor is the first sensation that runs through my waking body, my eyes looking down at the knife still buried in my chest, somehow missing vitals as strength and anger fills me. Hands grasp the handle and with a scream I pull it free, the wound inexplicably disappearing with it.

"What a day, of all the people to meet…" I huffed as I got to my knees, an inmate closing in on me with claws bared. I looked to Nestor, still on the ground and holding off Buck. "Hey, don't hold back. He still has a skull fracture from an old hunt, headbutt him with everything you have between the eyes and he'll go out like a light. Don't think, do it! And throw me my iPod!"

At the same time Nestor reared his head back to collide with the still confused Buck, the inmate lunged for me with a knife in hand. Rolling back and onto my feet, I tripped his lead leg and grabbed his head with my free hand, using his momentum to drive his body skull first into the hard concrete, my steel toe-capped boot coming down hard on his neck to silence him for good. Grabbing the iPod from Nestor, I saw it still playing as I put my headphones in. The next song to come up brought a smile to my face. I took the moment to call out to the prison, seeing a black shape in the distance.

"I realise Father up high called for my capture and my friend's demise, said he'd let you all go if successful… but he didn't tell you who I was. What I am."

Edgar flew overhead and dropped a cloth package down in my outstretched hand. I clasped it tight, the bandages unfurling, to reveal a beautiful scythe glistening under the alarm lights. Nestor held out his arm for the tired corvid as his other dragged Buck to the safety of the open cell, a smile on his face.

"I'm Nelle fucking Lockwood. The Last Sin Eater. And every one of you…" I twirled the scythe around toward them, confidence surging through me and meshing with the deep-seated fear. "…is about to be devoured."

Shutting the world out of its screams, insults, and drivel was always something I'd been adept at. Be it remarks of racism, sexism, or general bigotry, I grew immune to them. Music and focus went hand in hand for me. I wish I could tell you that I acted in grace, that I was quick-witted and full of candour.

But no, I'd devoured the sins of this prison and I was embodying every single one of them as I struck inmate after inmate in my pursuit of keeping those I loved safe. I acted as if Lady Death was watching and keeping score beside me.

My lust for victory, my greed for competition, my envy of all these worthless fools who had already lost their chance at redemption and not a care in the world beyond basic instincts, my sloth in the inability, deep down, to change anything meaningful and allowing this sickness to grow… my gluttony in wanting more time with Buck and my mother… my pride in my abilities, and the sickness of knowing where my genetics sprang from.

So many bodies rushed toward me, not the least bit deterred by my bravado or threats. That's fine, I would reap every single one if it meant I can save Buck. I don't care if it's fifty, one hundred, or ten thousand souls I have to take. Not a single one of them is worth Buck.

You can't save him.

No, shut up, I can. I just need to take them all out. A flip over the tall one, turn and thrust to take his head off and the torso of his friend, step aside from the incoming haymaker and rolling boot to the face. I could do this, I could.

There's too many. You will grow tired.

Fuck you, stop it. Just stop it. I'm not willing to give in. A dozen more, gone. This blade instilled me with the strength of ten Nelles!

And yet, it still won't be enough.

The internal battle raged on as I chipped away at the sea of violent offenders. The crowd overwhelmed me and piled on top as their pressure threatened to take everything I had.

"Shit, Lady Death helped you out, huh? Well, guess that means I can take off the restraints!" Nestor called out from above the pile of bodies. "Memento Mori."

In an instant, the bodies were thrown into the air and scattered in multiple directions, some hanging over the railings forty feet above us, others crumpled into a heap. As one larger man broke ranks and ran at me with a shiv, Nestor darted in front and with one uproarious kick to the man's neck, sent him hurtling into the concrete wall. He smashed into it with such force that small cracks formed around his impact.

Nestor looked bigger, tougher than he usually did. Arms beefier, and standing a little taller, Edgar by his side and clearly larger. On Nestor's black-gloved hands were obsidian knuckle dusters, his legs covered in thick pads.

"A phrase I was told only to use if things got dire and a sign was given. I guess this is it. You take care of father dearest, I've got the riff-raff!" He threw another haymaker, and the crowd was knocked back like a tidal wave. "GO! I'll join you when I can!"

A nod of gratitude given, I dashed past the still conscious prisoners and the cell, looking in for a moment to see if Buck remained unconscious. The look filled me with more dread than anything thrown at me in the prison.

The cell was empty.

No time to stop, I just had to hope he'd come to his senses and gone ahead. I saw the tulpa sins marching toward me, each of them nothing more than a facsimile of their sinners. Threatening, yes, but not worth my attention when Nestor and Edgar were so capable.

As I ran closer, scythe at the ready, I saw Edgar swoop in and cover the way with his black wings.

"Protect Mama. Protect Papa. Kill Corpse Hoarder."

"I will, honey. I will." I darted around as he screeched and caused a distraction, diving between outstretched hands and hungry mouths to reach the side of the building and scale the stairs.

In just a few moments, I'd be able to put this to an end.

Kicking open the doors to the warden's office, I expected immediate raised voices, a clash of blades and a quick resolution. Naive, I know.

Instead, I found myself rooted to the floor as the door slammed shut and the lights went out, matching the obscurity I'd seen on the outside just a short time ago.

"Ah, Nelle, this isn't how I wanted us to finally reunite, you know. I was hoping you'd have come to me with open arms and we'd be doing what needed to be done in order to bring this place to its foregone conclusion."

A shadow scuttled around me, the pale visage of the warden barely visible as my eyes adjusted.

"I want this over, Warden… All Father… whatever you call yourself. Nobody else has to get hurt."

He cackled. My body still not responding to my desire to move, I felt him walk closer, hands clasped around his face.

His eyes were bulging out of their sockets, flesh peeling away, shedding, as the black skin bubbled underneath. His hair steadily fell out with every step.

"You can't stop what's in motion, my sweet Nellie. Your mother couldn't stop it, neither can you. Who'd have thought that my own kin would work so hard to go against me? I thought after absorbing all these sins, you'd come to me willingly… but it seems your pride needs some extra work." He leaned in and I saw something amorphous behind him. Long, spindly limbs jutted out his back, pinning themselves to the far walls, and something grotesque on its shrouded face undulated as he smiled.

"Go fuck yourself. I have no father!" I spat, venom in my words as the scythe dropped from my hand and was kicked out of sight.

"Oh, that's where you're wrong, my love. *All* have a Father. You're just fortunate enough to share my lineage, but you may as well stop now. I have the prime reason for giving in with me right here…"

He clapped his hands and Buck walked into my field of view, mechanical and almost zombified in nature. His forehead still gushed blood and his eyes were shot through with red. The All Father put his hands on Buck's shoulders and patted them proudly.

"Your boy has my pride trigger in his soul. We both know removing a sin requires you to devour it. That, of course, requires time—time you do not have. So, here comes your final test, Nellie. Are you ready to do what must be done to help bring Sturgeon and this world to its rightful makers?"

He pushed Buck to his knees and placed a hand on his head. Buck's eyes rolled in the back of his head.

"STOP IT! PLEASE!" I begged, watching Buck's nose bleed profusely as All Father's smile grew wider, more monstrous.

"You may not have eaten your mother's sin, but you took off the emotional shackles she placed before falling into the void, one half of my restraints here. The other was put into those godforsaken totems and…" He lifted his hand and placed the other on my face, a searing, blinding pain rippling through every cell in my body. "In the two of you. The pride of the McGraw's and the pride of the Sin Eaters. Pitiful."

He let go and my body collapsed to the floor, head resting on the soft carpet in a daze as he knelt down to look at us both.

"He's going to wake up any moment now and become the next representation of pride. A great beast that will tear through everything until he finds a worthy host. You… well, you're still my daughter—you'll live. So your choice will be made. Follow me, stop me as your mother once tried, or stop the man you love. I certainly wouldn't wish to be in your shoes, that's for sure!" He walked toward the door and looked back, the horrific visage from my nightmares trailing behind him, almost melding with him as more of his skin broke away and something otherworldly poked out from underneath. He was changing rapidly. "Do you know why I chose the last name Leichenberg, Nellie? It means mountain of corpses. So many have tried to stop me in this life and others… they always fail. Don't make the same mistake. I look forward to the next family reunion."

I looked over at Buck, his eyes twitching. The dim light in the room showed me Nestor and Edgar battling hard to buy us time, but they'd tire before long. The inmates were unrelenting, and the tulpas were closing in.

"Th… b… ne…" I muttered. The warden's body tensed up and paused as he debated leaving me there.

"What was that? You'll need to speak up. This form has limited hearing."

"I... I'll join you if you help me up." I croaked, my shame overwhelming me. He shook in place, almost giddy.

"You're not lying, I can tell. Well, far be it from me to deny my brightest daughter. Come, come, let me help you!"

He picked me up and embraced me in a deep, loving hug. I could smell the decay on him, rot and sulphur with a meal of mushrooms and fruit manifesting near him in a golden bowl.

"I'm so proud of you, Nellie. I'd hoped you'd see sense. You'll be overjoyed to be there for the ascension!"

"There won't be one, Father."

Pulling my serrated blade from my holster, I dug it into his back. The wind exhaled from him as I held him close. His arms flailed, and he scratched at me to get away as I soothed him. A few seconds passed before I pulled it out and slashed his throat.

He gurgled for a second before black blood left his neck and he clutched wildly at anything in the room for support. I walked past him to the bowl and began devouring the decadent fruit, ganache cake, and mushrooms. I ate them with speed as his eyes widened and he pointed to me with a shaky finger.

"Pride... comes before... the fall..." He uttered, his body slumping to the floor, face down and motionless.

He was dead.

I rushed to Buck to pull him up, away from the body and to the entrance, begging him to open his eyes.

"Hey! Buck, honey, you gotta open your eyes, please!"

I had his head in my lap as we sat against the open door, hoping he'd open his eyes once more.

"I beat the odds, we can go home, you just need to..." I stopped mid-sentence. A cracking sound was coming from the spot where All Father laid.

His back hunched over and his skin continued to blacken and flake.

He was changing, like a chrysalis.

"You... you can't always win, Nelle."

I looked down and saw Buck, eyes open and full of fear. My hand stroked his hair softly as fear rather than relief mounted in me. "Something... something is wrong within me. Whatever the hell the warden did to me, it's screaming in my brain and I... I can't..."

His fists were clenched, and he bit his lip until it bled. He was resisting with everything he had.

"Oh, oh Buck... not like this... please..."

The warden's body continued to writhe, slowly losing its hue and cracking. We had minutes at most.

"Flesssshhh... prrriiissonnnn..." The distorted voice called, something unholy breaking away from the skin. I felt my anxiety mount, and Buck began thrashing at the mere calling of its voice like a moth to an evil flame.

Then, as if right on cue, my iPod started playing the last song on the playlist and I felt my world shatter. The delicate piano tones echoed from my headphones in the quiet chambers. Buck stopped thrashing and his pupils dilated, coming to his senses again.

"I need you to do something for me, Nelle. If this... thing inside me gets out. We're back to square one. But, with my compendium and all the knowledge I have up in this head, he's going to be even more dangerous. We can't let him out of here." He put his hand on mine and looked at me—truly looked at me. "You need to put an end to it. Now."

This was what Lady Death had warned me of. The price that would need to be paid. The sacrifice of one to stop the slaughter of many.

Tears filled my eyes and everything I had kept locked up started to fall out of me like a piece of fine china shattering on the ground, millions of fragments erupting everywhere, never able to be assembled properly again.

"Buck, I'm so lucky to have known you. You were my mentor, my friend... my everything." I stroked his face, trying to memorise the ruggedness of his chin, the small scar by his right eye, the softness of his hair. "I will carry you with me, always."

He simply smiled and took an earphone from me, putting it in his ear, and closing his eyes.

"Not a bad way to go, all things considered. We had an adventure, shared some stories and most of all... I got to lay in your arms." He breathed in once and lay still. "I love you, Nelle Lockwoo—"

I clasped my hands around his throat and pressed my thumbs into his windpipe with everything I had. He didn't resist until his survival reflexes kicked in. He pushed his body up and twisted it.

Anything to shake me off, hands clasping at me aimlessly. But he was still weak—and he'd taught me well.

Tears stained my face and fell onto his as I screamed. I screamed louder than anything I had ever mustered in my life. Every ounce of my sorrow was flowing through my hands and snuffing the light that was Simon McGraw out.

"I... Love... You... Nel—" He gasped, his eyes rolling into the back of his head as his body fell limp, starved of oxygen. I didn't relent as my eyes turned to the now emerging shape from the office, pain-wracked moans and hoarse whispers all I had left.

I would not let this thing take him. Not in a million fucking years.

"I am free of this flesh prison. I will be the doorway I was meant to be, so sayeth AMOS!" It screeched, bursting through the roof and perching itself on top, emitting horrifying sounds as it expanded and lit up the prison with its terrifying abilities.

I only let go when I knew his brain was completely starved of oxygen. Laying him down, I shut his eyes and kissed his forehead softly.

"I know you did, Buck. I know you did."

Ensuring his body was comfortable, I turned to rush down the hallway.

Leaving my love behind.

-

Turning onto the main floor, I no longer saw a fierce battle, no enemies in sight. Nestor simply pointed up. I saw the horror of a large unspeakable form with an almost spider-like face, large powerful limbs, and innumerable eyes. It cast its figure upwards as an arc of black light shot up through the prison. The tulpas of the sins stood around it in a prayer circle.

"Where's Buck? We gotta fucking go!" He called over the noise and carnage.

I looked to the office, tears running anew, and a smile on my face as I gave thanks to Lady Death. Buck's tulpa, scythe in hand, charged toward Amos with destruction in mind.

"Finishing the job." I replied, grabbing Nestor's hand and running for the exit.

With ungodly force, Buck's tulpa swung the scythe at the other manifestations, cleaving them in two before smashing Amos into a concrete pillar, collapsing it and causing a breach that rapidly filled the prison with water.

We'd made it to the elevator and pushed the emergency button as the staff still ran about as aimlessly as the other inmates, when a great roar rang out below us. Whatever was happening, it was escalating. Anxiety mounted in the three of us as the elevator climbed.

"Hey, Stian! Get your drunken ass over here, pronto! We've got a situation!" He yelled into his phone.

"Aye, I've been made aware. Landing in five. Is Madame listening?" His gruff, oddly melancholy voice called back. Nestor confirmed, and he continued speaking;

"And the stately ships go on
To their haven under the hill;
But O, for the touch of a vanish'd hand,
And the sound of a voice that is still!"

The elevator reached the entrance, and we made a dash for the exit. A huge blackened tendril smashed at the elevator shaft, and a guttural roar followed that chilled me to the bone. A mass with eyes began crawling out of the hole it had made.

"I am... the doorway... and it will be... opened!" It bellowed, the horrifying cacophony of inhuman vocal arrangements chilling my blood, before it was dragged back down and into a furious battle below.

"Not today, it won't. Goodbye, Father." We ran for the landing pad, jumping onto the plane as it took off. I glanced out at the scene of Tempestra Prison. It was filling with water, and a raging storm roared around it, fitting the destructive nature the institute had wrought on us all.

"Break, break, break, at the foot of thy crags, O Sea!" Stian called out as we made distance. As the structure sunk beneath the sea, a thick light shone out from underneath as if a depth charge had gone off, the entire building sinking into a huge whirlpool as lightning and high waves engulfed the area. Stian finishing his sombre poem with some of the most appropriate lines I'd ever heard:

*"But the tender grace of a day that is dead
Will never come back to me."*

—

The first two weeks after losing Buck were incomprehensibly tough. Everywhere I went, I was reminded of him, from the accomplishments reminisced upon by colleagues learning of his passing, to the many upstarts in Sturgeon he'd inspired. I stopped going out. I stopped doing much of anything that wasn't drinking or crying.

On the fifteenth night, a knock rang out and refused to cease until I answered it. I dragged myself from the study where I'd made a yurt of old memories and a sleeping bag, just to be near Buck's things and his scent. I put on my clothes and answered the door, fully ready to cast out whichever inconsiderate ass had disturbed my rest.

Looking through the peephole, I saw nothing save for the faint glimmering light of the lantern slinking back into the darkness. As I opened the door, a small note had been left.

"Tomorrow at midnight. Memento Mori. - L. D."

I slept feverishly during the day, making sure I looked and felt the part for a long journey. After the first trip on Caracossa Airways, I knew I'd need the energy. For some reason, I always felt the need to dress up for an occasion—something my grandparents instilled in me, I suppose.

Even if I was going to something unexpected and entirely unwanted.

Nestor met me at the entrance to our establishment, taking note of the FOR SALE sign in our front garden.

"Going anywhere nice, Nelle?"

"Mm, not sure. Maybe a little place by the beach, I know of a nice coffee shop that's on sale in the entertainment area, somewhere just between the spaces… I hear there's a dentistry far from Sturgeon where all manner of beasts and nightmares gather to get themselves fixed up. Maybe I can find a genie among them to grant my wish…"

I sniffed, shaking my head at my own stupidity. "Who am I kidding, it's a one-way trip. Nothing more to it."

"I wouldn't say it's quite that simple. Come on, Lady Death wanted to talk to you and there's a very excitable idiot son of mine that wants to preen you."

I chuckled, and he put his arm around me like a big brother as we got into a taxi and headed for the landing pad where the plane sat. While we were in transit, Nestor told me to shut my eyes while he applied some face paint, saying it was "necessary for the night's rites." Lord knows what that meant. Edgar sat in my lap in the car, still and expectant for the journey, cawing softly and occasionally saying:

"Mama. Time. Precious."

As if he knew what was coming.

I'm not totally sure what I expected when I boarded, but a soft orange light, beautifully painted skulls, and marigolds lining the entrance with fairy lights was not it.

"Dia De Los Muertos... of course." I sighed, taking in the majesty of the plane, walking down the aisle to near the front. "Nestor, aren't you busy tonight? Need some help with unruly passengers?"

I shook as the plane began its soft ascent, heading for the nearby ocean and travelling across it.

"Oh, I don't think I'm all that unruly, just a bit cheeky when I've had some wine, love!" A kind voice rang out from the furthest front row, that hair in the same bun from before. As she stood up, I saw her properly for the first time. She was older, the tiredness across her face and still irradiating beauty I'd admired as a little girl.

"Mum, I thought you'd..." I choked. She walked down the aisle toward me.

"You thought you'd killed me—or what was left of me in that prison—that you'd never get to see me again. Well, sorry to disappoint!" she laughed and held out her arms, letting them drop with an audible slap. She was real. "I'm still here. I was there, too, but not the same. The warden... Amos, as he is truly known, is a remarkably gifted creature. Always was, I suppose. With his own pride disease riddling you, he knew you could be weakened. Who better to use than me? Oh, I tried to resist, but so much of me was lost in that place, that there was so little left. But I remember what we talked about, I remember what we promised. And I still mean it, Eleanor." Mum stepped forward and her hand brushed my face, my heart sinking into my stomach at the realisation this truly was her. "I missed you, so very much. I'm so glad I could see you again, one last time."

Words failed me spectacularly, and when looking at myself in the mirror, I saw the skull makeup adorning my face. I turned and hugged my mother with everything I had, nestling myself in her, evoking those securities long lost from my childhood.

"I owed you a courtesy and a favour, Nelle. I keep my word, always." A soft, alluring voice called from the cockpit. Stepping out of the shadows, a long gloved arm holding a flame in her hand was Lady Death. No longer a skeletal figure but instead a beautiful young woman. Her face was hidden behind intricate skull makeup, and she was quite the alluring figure as she walked toward us. Mum parted with me to let her pass. "You fought for so long, you were owed, *are* owed a kindness. But, I must admit to something…" She gestured for me to take a seat opposite her, I obliged.

"There's a reason Nestor and Edgar were tasked with assisting us, isn't there?" I asked. Speaking plainly was all I had left at this stage. She nodded, and the flame opened to show the same deaths of those I didn't know but somehow loved.

"You changed the cycle, in ways that I cannot fully foresee. But, so much lays ahead of you now as the guide. Your path will be a difficult one, Nelle. It is owed to you as the daughter of the unbounded to know this before you embark on it." She took in a breath and shook her head as the images in the flame shifted again. "So many cycles in so many places, all of which you will come to know directly or indirectly as their guide: a bar between spaces, a hotel of alternate worlds, a mortuary that dissects anomalies and scourges… an estate with prophetic tarot cards, a home to childhood secrets in Static, a battleground of nightmares, and then…"

I saw an older me, standing in front of a creature of bone and malice, shrouded in locusts and charging toward my currents self, arms outstretched.

"…Death. You bring the cycle and go out with it. Great change goes through you, Nelle."

I gulped, unease setting in but unsure of how to process it, my head feeling foggy.

"I... is that the end of me? There in that pit?" I clutched at my skull as it burned.

"You cannot retain what I show you. This is a kindness I offer that you will hold in your subconscious, only coming to the surface when your time nears. To what end you are dead, I cannot say. But when you are close, you will know. I wanted you to know this path before you set off on it. And to give you an easier start. Memento Mori, Nelle Lockwood. Nobody does it alone."

As if on cue, I heard the trudging of steps from the lower level and the unmistakable frame of Buck. The glimmer of the moonlight cascading down on the ocean and refracting through the windows basked him in a glow that made him look downright radiant.

He smiled. I smiled. The simplest exchange imaginable.

Then we ran toward each other and kissed. The kind of kiss that comes along once in a lifetime. A first time kiss with someone you'd known and loved for years, an "I do" kiss at a wedding where one of the participants has limited time, an "I'll see you soon" kiss when you know it's not possible. A kiss that steals as many moments as it gives.

"I told you it'd all work out, didn't I?" He said, grinning, eyes glistening in the light. "I got my tulpa, grabbed the scythe—thanks, L. D.—smashed those weirdos into the next dimension and poof... here I am."

"Simon Buck McGraw, you still live up to your name even in death, don't you?" I pressed my head against his, laughing at first but then breaking into tears. "This is really it, isn't it? You're the sin I will carry, the one I can never devour."

"Yeah. I am." He said simply, his voice hoarse and full of regret. "I will always be with you. No matter where you go and what you do on the hunt. I'll be there..."

The plane started to slow as the orange lights grew in brightness, the outside turning to black. We'd reached the end.

"...Until you're ready to come home." His voice cracked with pain, tears in his eyes as we held one another for a while. When he broke away, he grabbed something from his bag.

"Are you giving me an engagement ring, Buck?" I jested, trying anything to keep the mood light in these final moments, my heart shattering with every passing second. He sniffed and shook his head.

"Nah, I'm giving you something more important and binding… The compendium. I'm the last keeper, the last McGraw. You're The Last Sin Eater, it seems fitting to me and only right that you should have it." He placed it in my hands and kissed my forehead. "It's all on you, now. Until we're reunited."

Mum walked over and did the same, passing me one of her rings as she did so.

"I'll be waiting for you. We'll have that Sunday Roast. I promise."

I stood there, unable to do anything as they walked to the exit. Lady Death stood by to place wreaths of magnolia flowers around their wrists. She whispered something in their ears, kissing them on the cheek as they passed over.

The blinding light filled the front of the plane, but neither of them seemed deterred as they smiled.

My last image of Buck and my mum walking off the threshold was that of pure joy. Four words escaped Buck's lips before the door closed, and I bid goodbye to the two most important people in my life.

"Oh, I'm finally home…"

Epilogue

This is the cycle. Two great sides sat on opposite ends of a long table, similar passionate goals, but completely different perspectives on how to achieve them based on where they sit.

One forgets, the other regrets.

I realise this is cliche, but this is by no means the end. Amos is a threat that was not quelled here, nor was Buck's indomitable spirit and drive to do what was right. As we look to our next tale: "The Spaces In Between," we see how things take shape some years later and another cycle begins. I of course will be there, as I am always there in some form or another. It is the nature of things for me to guide, partake and observe, destined to be chained to this until an end can be reached.

For there are still other threads to unravel, other members of the cycle still needing help against equally terrifying scourges in Sturgeon. Until they're protected, educated, and brought to the fight against The Unbounded, I won't ever stop. I cannot stop.

Because I'm The Last Sin Eater.

I'm the keeper of The Cryptid Compendium.

I'm Nelle Lockwood.

And the cycle begins and ends with me.

Acknowledgements

Mum and Dad, who gave me the most important typewriter a six-year-old could ever have. You have always been supportive, and I am nothing without you both. To know Dad lived to see this happen makes my heart swell like nothing else. I love you both very much.

Jerry, Jai, Ashley: I would not be sane or able to keep it together without you throughout the past twelve months. Constant check-ins, heart-to-hearts, and leaning on each other brings us all to greater successes. You are my brothers and I know what each of you will do in the business as the years go on—we will change things together.

Mark, Sam, Des, Kay, Nat, Dev, Handley, Jordy, Dominick, Leah, Hanmer: Thank you for always providing a safe place for me to go mentally when things got too much on the writing front, a positive gaming culture, and making me laugh so much it frequently brought tears to my eyes.

Tim, Olie, Kev, Khan, Ashe, Paddy, Chris: I appreciate you boys more than words can say. Even without wrestling right now, you keep me so grounded. Thank you for always being there to talk to. PTB.

Kieran: You are one of the most amazing humans I have ever met. You've saved my ass more times than I can count and ensured I can keep doing this when I felt I could no longer persist. I will never be able to thank you enough for what you've done, but I hope I can continue to be a person you and Leah are proud of.

My NoSleep family: Chrissi, Lair, Olivia, David, Brandon, Alexandra, Dan Z, Gemma, Michael, Roo, Penny, Marni, Ronnie, Max, Laura, Hannah, Gerden, Rehn, Patrick, Rebecca, Daria, Ethan, Alynda, Nick B., Bonnie, Wil, Elias, C. K., Nick M., Tor, Melodi, Natalie, Gabi, and *so* many others: Both professionally and personally, I am a better person for meeting you all. Thank you for putting up with me and providing nothing but good vibes and great feedback. None of this is possible without you.

David and Olivia: For giving me the opportunity to expand on my existing skills, meet a new audience, and take my career to new heights, I will never be able to repay the gratitude I have. NSP is one of the absolute greatest teams I have been privileged to work for and with. I will champion both them and the two of you whenever I have the chance. Thank you.

Rom and Ronnie: This wouldn't have reached anywhere near as many people without the initial adaptation, the constant support to adapt the existing content, and now a thriving fandom that is eager for more. This success is yours as much as mine. I love you both.

Erika and Mark: My production and acting siblings. How many times have you sat and listened to me prattle on over the last six months, I wonder? I wouldn't be the performer, writer, or man I am without your constant guidance. Thank you from the bottom of my heart. Big ups to Shadows At The Door, and Unbound Theatre!

Andy: I fuckin' did it, man. Now go make millions with your comic series, thanks for always standing by me. I love you, buddy.

Qachina and Avery, who saw most of my work in its earliest phases when I was on my own and finding my feet with this "full time writing" lark: Your help cannot be understated. It would not be what it is without you. You are both remarkable women.

Special thanks to Angela who provided the endorsement on the back of this novella. You are an unbelievably kind person who gave up so much time to me and helped me figure out how to take my craft to the next level. I hope to one day get the accolades you have achieved. I am grateful for your friendship. Thank you.

Special thanks to Bonnie and Patrick for helping with the formatting, Emily for the AMAZING artwork, and to Rebecca, our tireless editor. This novella does not exist without you.

Special thanks to my manager Marc at WBE. You have been an amazing person to learn from the past couple years and I wouldn't have gotten this far without your wisdom and belief in my abilities. The fact you took a chance on me is something I will NEVER forget. I hope I continue to do you proud, buddy.

To everyone we lost, those we couldn't save, and those who are at peace after a lifelong war with their demons: You will always be loved and you will always be honoured.

To all of you who preordered: Be it in kindle format, physical copy, or signed… Thank you for believing in me.

And for Clara, my little light who will live forever. This is for you. I will always love you.

T. J. Lea

<u>Bonus Story</u>

This ending little tale is an exclusive addition and a (potential) start to a later entry in the Sturgeon mythos detailing Nestor and Edgar's job as security detail for the dead. Eagle-eyed fans will have recalled this conversation earlier in The Last Sin Eater. It felt apt to include it.

If you like it, I hope to hear your thoughts. Perhaps it will be fleshed out for year two…

- TJ

T. J. Lea

The Ferry of the Dead

Everyone thinks their job is strange, stressful, or downright unbearable at times, right?

Well, few end up doing what I'm doing—that is, standing in the workers break room, a paltry little shoebox next to the cockpit, wiping brain matter bone off of their uniform while their corvid Edgar repeatedly shouts "SNAP! SNAP! SNAP!" on your shoulder. A room of identical passengers all stood chanting in the aisle while your driver loudly, and drunkenly, quotes Lord Tennyson by heart and your engineer chomps down on a brick, maniacally screaming between bites, "The water-bears are getting restless!"

This is an average flight for us, but it's the one that spurred me on to telling you all about what we do and how it led to this point.

I've worked this gig for the past three years and it's only now when things are chaotic that I realise the importance of sharing this in the hopes that someone out there has heard of us before. We don't get that many passengers anymore, owing to competition from rival afterlife travel services, and most folks not having the correct currency on them when they die.

My decision to document this is that maybe, just maybe, it'll jog someone's memory.

Have you heard of Caracossa Airways?

I guess I should start from the beginning. My name is Nestor Holden and I'm an Air Marshal for a water flight service known as Caracossa Airways. The airline company originally tried going by simply "Charon" but their marketing went down the drain, probably for the best. The spirit of our job is entrenched in that word: Charon. The legendary ferryman who ensured the lost souls got to the underworld safely so long as they paid him a coin. Times have progressed, but the sentiment hasn't. People still need transporting to their respective afterlife; there's just far more of them now. Adapt or perish is the rule of the world, and even the land of the dead must abide by it. My job is to ensure those trips are safe and without major incident.

I should make a couple things clear from the outset: we don't have an "airport," so to speak, folks tend to just appear in their assigned seats when we're on the way back from the last trip. Neither myself nor the staff are technically dead—I realise that's a loaded statement but you'll have to trust me on that one for now.

Naturally, you get your usual issues when ferrying people from one plane of existence to the other. Those who won't accept it and try to accost you to get back to the other side, violent offenders who are every bit the scumbag in death that they were in life, that sorta thing.

It used to be rare that you encountered something beyond the norm, something that called upon you to act in unusual ways.

It was a midnight run. I was speaking with the pilot Stian, an older man with a barrel chest fit for holding the ungodly amounts of liquor he'd pour down his gullet, staining his brown beard. You'd look at him and immediately get a strong sense of confusion—the man looked physically fit but had the gait of someone whose soul was, no pun intended, in limbo. His brown eyes would glaze over, regret filling them as he took a hefty swig of whiskey, before laughing and espousing British poetry over the intercom in an attempt to placate our guests. Still, when he was lucid, he was a brilliant man with a wicked sense of humour.

"Christ, how many more runs do we have before L. D. gives us our time off?" I groaned, rubbing my neck and feeling the strain in my muscles, eyes stinging from exhaustion but thankful for the dim blue light filling the plane.

"Eh, you know how the boss is. If there's an influx in tragedy and nobody else nearby, we've just gotta keep going. Ain't much more for it, Chief." He chuckled, taking a quick swig as the moonlight shone on the nose of the plane, illuminating the beautiful Black Sea beneath us. "By the way, your bird was talking in my ear again while you were making dinner, when are you gonna train that thing?"

I looked to my shoulder and stared at Edgar. He was a crow I'd had since I joined up with Carcossa. They told me he was an "emotional support bird," they just didn't specify the emotions. He cocked his head when I looked at him and uttered, "Oh hi, what's up?" His eyes darted around the room and centred on Stian.

"Did you tell him to crash the plane again, Edgar?" I asked, narrowing my eyes, suspicion growing as he refused to meet my gaze. "What did we say about being a devil's advocate?"

Edgar bowed his head solemnly, muttering "Not enough pay," to the delight of Stian, chuckling heartily and stroking his head, calling him a "smart bird."

"Corvids aren't supposed to be that good at talking, you know."

I turned and saw a young girl standing in the aisle, hands behind her head, observing the three of us as Stian waved dismissively for us to shut the door on him. I obliged before turning back and smiling at our inquisitive passenger.

"You know he's a corvid just by looking at him, huh?" I said, smiling. She nodded and craned her neck to look at Edgar more, busy preening himself and paying no mind. "Clever, what's your name?"

"Bryanna Higgs. And yours?"

"Nestor. This here's Edgar. I'm the air marshal, just a glorified peacekeeper on this tin bucket. How d'you know Edgar here is a corvid?"

Bryanna smiled. "We studied them in eighth grade biology. They're good at mimicry but they're not meant to have conversations."

I looked at him and shrugged, rubbing my hand across my five o'clock shadow. "Edgar's different, I guess. But he still has a mind of his own and rarely does whatever I say."

"WEIRDO ALERT! WEIRDO ALERT!" He cried, flapping his wings and unceremoniously knocking against my face. I remained still, used to him by this point as I held out a hand saying "See?" and expecting a laugh.

Bryanna's eyes widened, and her demeanour shifted. She lowered her hands from behind her head and her voice dropped to a whisper.

"Nestor, I need to ask you something… have you ever done something you regret?" I saw myself reflected in her glasses and thought back to the countless times I'd told someone I loved them when I was merely in the early stages of infatuation, when I'd cheat on a video game to satiate my ego, or the countless times I'd boasted about my skills beyond their actual boundaries just to gain some clout.

"Sure, once or twice. Why?" I inquired, curious as to why her personality shifted so quickly. She ignored me and asked another question.

"And have you ever had someone you couldn't help but listen to? Like… an imaginary friend?"

Again, I took a minute to think about my childhood. My imaginary friend was a stuffed animal that frequently told me dirty jokes and encouraged my passion for drawing stick figure wars on my bedroom walls.

"Yeah, I had one of those too. Did you?"

She nodded nervously, refusing to move or take her eyes off of me. "He was special, I didn't even know what he looked like until… until the end. But he was weird looking, had a neck that was way too long, like a giraffe."

"A giraffe, huh? That's weird, but the imagination doesn't work logically, I guess. Any other questions?" Again, she nodded.

"How many other people are on this plane?" Her voice dropped lower, hands shaking as we stood in the aisle. I looked around and saw mostly empty seats. This was our midnight flight, and the numbers were even lower than usual.

"Five, maybe six? But they're all below deck, destined for one place and one place only. You're the only one up here."

Her eyes welled up, and she moved forward, taking my hand with hers and gripping it tightly as she motioned for me to crouch down and listen to her.

"Then why is the giraffe man from my imagination sitting over there?"

She stood behind me and gestured toward seat six, row fifteen. A tall, shrouded figure leaned against their window seat, comically long neck drooping forward as if sleeping. In an instant, I knew what it was. When a passenger passes into our plane, the essence of limbo, their unresolved feelings and regrets can manifest physically. In this case, I guess whatever happened to her followed her for the ride. Not that that's an immediate problem, mind you. My job isn't just to restrain unruly souls, it's helping excise their demons before we can drop them off at their destination.

All I could do for now was keep her calm, figure out what happened.

"Hey, do you wanna hold Edgar?" I asked, smiling as I took him on my wrist, his attention now focused on Bryanna and her glasses.

"Shiny, protective, tappable." He chimed, pecking at the lenses playfully but not trying to remove them. To her credit, Bryanna didn't flinch after the first tap, but held out a shaky hand to let him hop on.

"Don't worry, he doesn't steal many shiny objects anymore, he's just inquisitive. He's more likely to steal something basic and unnecessary than the glasses on your face." I gave her a reassuring smile as he hopped onto her wrist and she gently stroked his neck, still standing away from the far aisle as the gentle hum of the plane reflected the steady rise it took. A slight rocking sensation hit the aisle, and I motioned to her to sit down on the adjacent seats as the plane ascended.

"Only our pilot Stian knows the routes. Sometimes we never go off the ocean surface, sometimes we never land on it." I motion my hands around confusingly. "The routes he takes are... tough."

"He clasps the crag with crooked hands; Close to the sun in lonely lands," Stian's voice bellowed from the cockpit, my own chiming in with him as he continued on, eyes rolling in my head as he continued:

"'Ring'd with the azure world, he stands.' Yeah, Stian, I love The Eagle too..." I sighed, looking back to Bryanna, who had calmed down in the face of our cavalier nature. "He loves Lord Tennyson, our Stian. A few others, too, but that guy really speaks to him. Anyway, I need to ask you a couple of questions, is that okay?"

She nodded, her face fixated on my own as Edgar hummed in her lap. My own eyes occasionally darted to the unmoving shape in the far corner of the plane.

"Alright, do you know where we are right now? Where *you* are right now?"

She took a moment; her face tensing before she nodded. "I'm not alive anymore, am I?"

I shook my head, sighing. "Afraid not, but it's rare to meet even grown adults so relaxed about the whole thing... why are you not scared, asking to go home, or for your parents?"

Bryanna shrugged and stared at Edgar as she replied bluntly, "Wouldn't matter. If I'm dead, then I'm dead. Maybe it's a good thing."

"A good thing? Why would you…" I stopped, assessing the situation in front of me was vital and connecting the dots mattered, even if I didn't sense a threat. "You remember how you died, don't you?"

Her head stayed bowed, but I could sense tears as she sniffed and nodded.

"Would you mind telling me about what happened?"

She shuffled in her seat, using her long sweater sleeves to wipe her eyes underneath her glasses as Edgar quietly chimed "Pretty. Hollow. So much, so little." I sat down on the seat in the opposite aisle. A quick look toward our mutual concern in the far corner assured me he was staying put for the time being.

"Have you ever heard sounds in the dead of night that you can't explain, Nestor?" She asked quietly, her face angled down and focused entirely on Edgar.

"Of course, lots of people have. But I think most folks just hear their home settling, cars outside, or neighbours all the time." I reasoned, scratching my chin. "Not all that unusual when you put your mind to it."

She shook her head. "No, I mean when all those things aren't possible and the sound doesn't stop. It just continues droning on in your ear like you're hearing it underwater and can't ever make out what it is. It's both annoying and leaves you desperate to know what it is."

"Ah, well then no, not unless you count the ringing in your ears after a concert?" I mused, thinking back to when I saw My Morning Jacket some years ago. I continued. "It ruined my sleeping pattern for a whole two days after that. I drank so much coffee I couldn't function, too much shaking."

"Mine was like that, but it was voices. At first, I just thought it was maybe my own thoughts… I think it's called an internal monologue? But that's the thing, Nestor. I've never had such a thing."

I stare at her incredulously, her demeanour shifting.

"I can't fully explain how I form thoughts, but I don't have a voice in my head like you or most people do. Not until a few weeks ago. It started as muffled sounds and took everything I had to strain and capture the basic noises, but it was just too much. I remember one night I was trying so hard and a new voice rushed into my ears, he told me that I wasn't ready to understand what I could hear and that I would need dedication."

I sat there, small vocal affirmations to show I was listening but not wishing to interrupt her flow.

"He told me if I wanted to stop the noises, I needed to look inside myself in order for true understanding, that it would take everything I had and that it would set me free. I stopped sleeping and began focusing on whatever he told me to do, even if it meant upsetting my parents and my older brother. I was so determined to get the noise out of my head, Nestor. I had to do it, you need to believe me… I'm not a bad person." She pleaded, sniffing but still not making eye contact. The form in the corner shifted.

"The noise grew in intensity. It pulsed against my head and went beyond that of a standard migraine. I wasn't able to sleep, think, or function without the other voice in my head guiding me. He told me that if I wanted to take what he called 'the plunge' then I needed to do exactly as he said. He told me it would show me the truth and he would be free to guide me. When you're in that much pain, I think even grownups would do anything to be free of it."

She stopped petting Edgar and held her arm out for me to take him, her free hand rubbing her temple as I quickly set him back on my shoulder. His sounds fell silent as she continued.

"I rolled my eyes back as he instructed and, at his instruction, I pushed hard against my better judgment. He told me that the eyes were kept in their sockets as a seal on what lay behind, the connector between the flesh and the mind. He said I was special and that if I wanted to hear them clearly, I had to give it my all…"

She took off her glasses, and I felt my stomach contract. White orbs sat where full, vibrant eyes should be, rocking in their sockets and spinning as she spoke.

"The snapping was painful, but it was over quickly. I felt my vision blur and as they turned to face the darkness, I saw the tunnel before me, the voice urging me to look deeper. My eyes did as instructed, and I felt them rush as they descended, deeper and deeper as these colours flashed past me until my eyes again felt as if they were in sockets, hanging from a ceiling. Below me, I saw little creatures, far too many to count, all rushing through tunnels in my body and moving little substances around. The sounds of the rushing, Nestor... they were coming from something in the back of this cave, but it wasn't a cave, it was still me... I could see the surrounding walls pulsing with my heartbeat, my breathing creating an echo within the chamber."

The figure in the back rose from its seat, the long neck meeting the ceiling and crunching forward as the frame continued to stand up, the features still obscured as thin digits gripped the seats in front and dug their filthy nails into the leather. Edgar's head snapped up and stared at it, cawing and flapping his arms.

"It was a black, pulpy mass with teeth and no eyes. The rushing sound was its screaming growing more bold with each piece of me they fed it. I could see more than just one. There were *so* many eyes fixed on me, but they were too blurry to make out. I tried to move my eyes away, but I felt them being pulled in by these little creatures and added to the mass. I flailed and begged for it to stop, but I felt a thud in my chest and fell to my knees. The sounds of my parents screaming was the last thing I heard before I passed out..." She shuffled and pulled at her sleeves. "I swear, I'm a good person, Nestor. I loved my parents, really I did."

The figure began crawling over the seats, the head a good ten feet ahead of the rest of the body. Illuminated by the moonlight for a moment, I could see patchwork hair, skin stretched to the point of splitting, a smooth canvas where eyes and a nose should be, a mouth not filled with innumerable teeth as so many legends foretell, but jagged, darkened obelisks and stalactites that oozed a black fluid as it threatened to bear down on Bryanna.

"When I awoke, I could only make out shapes, but I knew what had happened. My stomach burned with a hole in the centre and I could hear my mother screaming as a wet, snapping sound gave way to a gurgle, then to silence. The pain was so bad, but it wasn't anything compared to the realisation of what I'd done."

I stood up, my hand reaching for my gun. This creature was getting too close, and I still didn't know enough to stop him.

"I'd set the voice in my head free and before everything went dark, he whispered in my ear..."

"Get me on that plane." The giraffe man screeched as it crawled forward, claws bared at me.

"Hey! Stian! We need some altitude!" I called, knowing I'd need to capture his interest. I ducked down low and shouted: *"The wrinkled sea beneath him crawls;"*

"He watches from his mountain walls!" Stian called back through the intercom as uproarious laughter filled the plane and the aisle steadily rose, the momentum carrying the giraffe man plummeting toward the far reaches of the plane.

"And like a thunderbolt he falls. You know, for once I'm grateful for Tennyson, Stian." I called back, knocking on the ceiling, laughter still ringing out.

I looked down at Bryanna, eyes still spinning and her breathing erratic. Holding onto the seats to steady myself, I called out over the tumultuous sounds of laughter, screeches, and engines roaring.

"Bryanna, there's something important you need to understand about being here. Anything you bring with you can become a creature; emotions can become monsters. Your regrets literally join you here until you deal with them." I looked back at the twisted form now below us, righting itself as it climbed. "But I'll give you credit, we rarely ever get anything as ugly as *that*."

"What do we do? I don't have a way to make him go away, Nestor." She cried, hands over her head. "He made me cut my father into little pieces to feed the beast inside me. He laughed as I flailed helplessly and drove the knife into him repeatedly. I couldn't see it, but I knew it was me. I deserve this, Nestor. I deserve whatever punishment I get!" She screamed and the giraffe man, now emboldened, took a leap toward us.

"Trust me on this, he is nothing more than your imaginary friend. I promise you that in this world there are few things that are absolute truths, but this is one of them." I took her hand despite the fact I knew I would slip. "You can trust me to keep you safe on your journey. You just have to believe that you are in charge of your destiny."

Her mouth fell open, but she nodded and sat up. "I won't be afraid, I trust you." Edgar flew off my shoulder to harass the creature, pecking at his face and pulling his hair while screeching "Neck too long! Creepy!"

The plane leveled out, and I walked toward it, adjusting my gloves with every step.

"You, my dear friend, are not normal. Not even by our measurements here at Caracossa. You are something entirely new. It's rare we see more than shadows, or maybe a projection of a passenger's past experience on these flights. So what makes you so special?"

The creature snapped its long neck and leaned forward, the body staying still while the head came within earshot. The voice was disarmingly elegant and raspy despite his gruesome mouth.

"There was a need to get on this plane, to find out who operated it. Whatever means necessary." He hissed as he twisted his head to observe Bryanna. I clicked my fingers at him.

"Hey, no. You're focusing on me. What did you hope to achieve? You realise how this works, right? Once she accepts her fate and gives you no more power, you're done. So you may as well explain yourself."

A vile grin spread across its face like a cancer as he uttered a phrase that would come to shake my core in the coming days.

"Reconnaissance for The Mortal Coil. There are more."

He shrieked again, preparing to strike before Bryanna stepped in front of me, arms outstretched.

"If you came from my mind and told me to do all those bad things, then you're my creation and I refuse to let you hurt anyone else! I won't let you scare me either!"

I stood there, transfixed, a hand on my gun as this monstrosity froze. The air left its lungs before it scratched at its throat and writhed on the floor, falling still after a few moments. Dead.

Bryanna breathed heavily and fell into her seat. Edgar sat pecking at the body on the floor and remarking "Dead. Creepy Man Dead." before flying back and perching on my shoulder.

-

After a few more hours, our flight landed and what little passengers we had disembarked, but not Bryanna.

"This isn't your stop." I said, smiling. "We have a little further to go for yours."

She looked perplexed, but I let her stroke Edgar again while we travelled for another hour as we discussed birds, biology, and monsters. I was just thankful she wasn't in pain or distress. Nobody so young should do this alone.

"This is your captain speaking, we're now arriving at our final stop of the evening. Miss Bryanna, this is for you." Stian's voice, now sober and lucid, broke over the intercom as he recited a part of another Tennyson poem:

> *"And the stately ships go on*
> *To their haven under the hill;*
> *But O for the touch of a vanish'd hand,*
> *And the sound of a voice that is still!"*

The plane came to a steady halt as I helped Bryanna to her feet. Edgar was now nestled and asleep on my head, making an utter mess of my hair. I couldn't tell you where his wings ended and my hair began.

"Where are we?" She asked, the door being pulled open. I looked out the window and smiled at her.

"Somewhere familiar." I replied.

"Break, break, break, at the foot of thy crags, O Sea!" Stian called over the intercom, the enthusiasm and wit gone from his voice as he recounted it quietly, but with unbridled passion.

Bryanna's eyes welled up as she stepped out into a room—her room.

"How... how is this... how am I..." she began, unable to find the words.

"Look, I'm just an air marshal. I don't know how any of it works. But my guess is the moment you accepted what happened, your suffering finally ended. And all this?" I gestured around the room from the airplane door frame. "This is your reward. The door here will disappear the moment we take off. I wouldn't try to figure out any of this... just think of it as your ever after."

"Is it... real? Am I back home with my family?" She asked, choking back tears.

"Hell, Bryanna. Does it matter? There are far worse fates out there, y'know." I scratched the back of my head, the muscles aching more now. "I say accept it, you never know what it could be."

She opened her mouth to reply, but her mother's dulcet tones called her from the other room.

"Bry! Honey! We're just starting game night, you coming? You know your dad will choose an awful character for you if you don't hurry!" To which her father jovially responded, "Hey! Dwarves are NOT awful! They're refined! Come on, Cap'n Bry! Adventure awaits!" before scoffing at his own joke.

She stifled a cry as she listened to her parents, not knowing if it was even real or not. She looked back at me one last time and whispered "Thank you" before leaving the room.

"Well damn, that was emotional. You know, when we started rising like that I was worried something would get straight up fucked, but you pulled through for us without damaging my ship… well, save for the seats!"

I turned to the source of the jubilant voice and saw my engineer, Calista, standing in the aisle. She was a fair-skinned twenty-something with a phenomenal understanding of mechanics and the inner-workings of the company. She was wise beyond her years but always falling short of understanding social cues and the timing for inappropriate jokes. Still, she was endearing, and it was hard not to like her, even as she munched down on a brick and stained her overalls. Calista had pica and insisted on a steady supply of bricks and water to keep her healthy. It took every bit of restraint L. D. had to not try to alter her tastes immediately. Eventually, Calista agreed to eat normal foods "if she must," but bricks were her go-to.

"I did what I could, but that was the most animated manifestation of someone's fears and regrets I've ever seen. Kid was intelligent, but to be that attuned to your emotions and make something like that? It's… just strange." I remarked, sitting down slowly so as not to wake up Edgar.

Calista moved over to where the body fell and looked down, frowning.

"Well, here's something that'll shock you—this guy is real." She replied simply before crouching and beginning to inspect the corpse.

"What? No, he came from inside her mind… literally. There's no way." I walked over and sure enough, a man in his late thirties lay there on the ground, face frozen in utter terror and teeth destroyed, but otherwise fully human.

"This… this isn't the same guy we fought. He had a giraffe-like neck, and claws. What the hell is this?"

"Well, either you're just fuckin' stupid and can't see the forest through the trees… or…"

"Or?" I motioned for her to continue.

"No, that's it. You're just not seeing the reality of it. You ever see folks wear animal skins to get close to their prey? Well, this is kind of like that. Whoever these people are, however they got through to our little Bryanna, they captured what terrified her and wore it. Clever way to get onto the plane, if you ask me." She sighed and hunched her shoulders. "This ain't the end of it either. I heard her over the audio feed, she said she saw more than one pair of eyes staring at her in there and ol' long neck here confirmed it." She shrugged. "We've got saboteurs, Nestor. Looks like you're gonna be busier around here." She picked up the body and took it back down to her workshop as I stood there, dumbstruck.

This would only be the first of many cases where horrors tried to take over Caracossa airways.

All I could do was stare as the last of Stian's poem rang out over the intercom, greeting the Black Sea once more:

"But the tender grace of a day that is dead
Will never come back to me."

About The Author:

T. J. Lea is a horror writer from Buckinghamshire, UK. He is best known for his creepypasta viral sensation "The Expressionless" back in 2012, though he has now moved onto creating the Sturgeon universe over on NoSleep through award winning content.

TJ is also known for his contributions to audio dramas such as the award winning NoSleep Podcast. He is the creator, host and co-producer of the NSP affiliated show The Writers Mythos and enjoys testing his voice acting skills on his YouTube narration channel "Dusklight Radio" whilst furthering his Sturgeon based universe in the process.

TJ's next entry into the Strangeness In Sturgeon series: *The Spaces In Between* will be released in the summer and is a direct continuation from The Last Sin Eater. He plans to release all six of his Year 1 arcs in 2021.

Tjaylea.com
Twitter.com/tjaylea
Reddit.com/r/tjaylea

Printed in Great Britain
by Amazon